The Winning Edge

The Winning Edge

Michele Martin Bossley

James Lorimer & Company Ltd., Publishers
Toronto

James Lorimer & Company Ltd. acknowledges the support of the Ontario Arts Council. We acknowledge the support of the Government of Canada through the Book Publishing Industry Development Program (BPIDP) for our publishing activities. We acknowledge the support of the Canada Council for the Arts for our publishing program. We acknowledge the support of the Government of Ontario through the Ontario Media Development Corporation's Ontario Book Initiative.

Cover illustration: Sharif Tarabay

Library and Archives Canada Cataloguing in Publication
Bossley, Michele Martin
        The winning edge

(Sports stories)
ISBN-13: 978-1-55028-637-3 (bound)
ISBN-10: 1-55028-637-4 (bound)
ISBN-13: 978-1-55028-636-6 (pbk.)
ISBN-10: 1-55028-636-6 (pbk.)

I. Title. II. Series: Sports stories (Toronto, Ont.).

PS8553.0794W56 1998   jC813.'54   C98-932337-4   PZ7.B67Wi 1998

James Lorimer & Company Ltd.,   Distributed in the United States by:
Publishers   Orca Book Publishers
317 Adelaide St. West   P.O. Box 468
Suite 1002   Custer, WA USA
Toronto, Ontario   98240-0468
M5V 1P9
www.lorimer.ca

Printed and bound in Canada.

CONTENTS

1 A Dream Come True 9

2 Making It Happen 15

3 The Royal Family 22

4 Jennie Skates 29

5 The Great Egg Incident 40

6 Double Trouble 50

7 An Extra Edge 56

8 My Ex-Best Friend 64

9 Rival at the Rink 71

10 Looking for Answers 80

11 Kallana and the Homework Patrol 89

12 Kate Takes Over   96

13 Amy Skates   101

14 Promise of a Dream   109

15 The Gold Medal   114

Thanks are due to Joan Crockatt, Jo Mark, Corryine Desouza and Kelly Mandryk for their suggestions pertaining to this book, to Scot Urquhart for his immeasurable help in retrieving this manuscript from a potential computer disaster, and especial thanks go to skating coach Shellie Davies, whose advice, enthusiasm and extensive knowledge of the sport of figure skating were integral in the writing of this book.

1 A Dream Come True

Mrble-mbb … mubble mmb-mub."

The voices were muffled through the office door. I pressed my ear cautiously against the wood. I was waiting for my dad after skating practice, and he was talking with Kate, my coach. I wasn't supposed to hear their conversation, but the temptation to eavesdrop was irresistible. I hadn't been goofing off in practice lately, so I didn't think I could be in trouble.

"Her composure under pressure … it's remarkable in someone her age." Kate's voice was clear enough to make out the words. Was she talking about me? I edged closer, my face mashed sideways against the door.

Kate coached figure skaters, both pairs and ladies singles. There were four other novice girls besides me, a few junior and senior skaters, and lots of younger skaters. We all belonged to Richmond Skate, one of Calgary's competitive figure skating clubs.

"There's an appeal, a charisma that Jennie has

when she skates, and it's the kind of thing that will make her an audience favourite. I'm telling you, Mr. Brewster, I've seen a lot of skaters and a lot of talent, but Jennie is ... or could be ... something special on that ice."

My jaw dropped in surprise. Kate never paid me those kind of compliments. In fact, no matter how hard I worked, Kate always found things I could improve in my skating. I was so dazed I missed my father's reply.

"No," Kate was saying. "I think we'll keep her basically on the same training schedule she has right now. But we have to adjust our thinking. If Jennie wants to become a top contender, it's time to start thinking that way. Technically, she needs to be stronger. She has the ability to advance to more difficult jumps, but we need to refine her moves. I would recommend putting her in an extra private lesson sometime after Christmas, and until then we'll continue as we are."

My father cleared his throat, scraped his chair legs against the floor and muttered something I could not hear. I waited for more, eager to know what else Kate had to say, when the door opened abruptly. Since I was leaning against it, with my head glued to the doorknob, I stumbled, almost landing in a dishevelled heap on the floor.

"Jennie!" my dad's face was red, either from embarrassment or anger — I couldn't tell.

Kate hid a grin. "Quite an entrance, Jennie. I think we'll have to work on being a little more graceful, though."

I could feel my cheeks burning. "I was waiting for you," I said, inventing rapidly. "But you were taking so long, I thought I'd just try and figure out how much longer you were going to be." They saw right through me.

"Sure you were," Dad said, taking my elbow and steering me out the door.

Kate leaned against the door frame and suppressed a chuckle. "See you at practice in the morning, Jennie."

I scooped up my skating bag under my father's glare and smiled back. "Five-thirty. Don't be late!" I said.

"Never!" Kate stepped back into the tiny office, and Dad and I hurried through the lobby.

"What did you think you were doing?" Dad said, stopping to zip up his jacket. He didn't sound angry, just exasperated.

"Nothing. I was just waiting, like I said. You were taking forever, and I'm starved. I want to get home."

"Me, too." He turned up his jacket collar and I did the same. I could see glittering beads of frozen rain flashing under the streetlights outside, and wet-black trees tossing their branches against the cold autumn wind.

"Ready?" Dad turned to me. "Let's run for it."

Clutching my skate bag in one hand and the front

of my jacket with the other, I dashed with him around the building to the parking lot and ran for the car.

"Hurry!" I cried, dancing from one foot to the other as my dad fumbled for the keys. He unlocked the doors and I slid inside. I brushed the cold rain from my face and shivered. September had been summer-warm, but October had blown in with a bluster of sleet and ice.

I get quite enough ice at the rink, thank you. I practice every day except Sundays, and twice a day Mondays, Tuesdays and Fridays, with sessions in the morning as well as after school. I don't need more ice from the weather, too. But in Calgary, we get our fair share of it in the winter.

Dad dropped into the driver's seat and turned the ignition.

"It'll take a few minutes for the car to heat up," he said, flipping on the windshield wipers. I wrapped my arms around myself to keep warm.

"So?" Dad asked.

"So what?" I said.

"Come on, Jennie. I know you heard everything Kate said. What do think about it?"

"Well … " I hesitated, then excitement bubbled up. "It's wonderful — I've been dreaming about this since I was a little kid. But it's kind of scary, too."

"Reality usually is." Dad braked for a red light.

I swallowed. "What do you mean?"

"Sometimes when you're faced with the real situation instead of the fantasy, it's scary because it might not turn out the way you think. In real life, there's always the risk of failure, but in dreams, you can make things turn out the way you want. Besides, real life is rarely perfect."

"Oh." I thought about that for a moment, then returned to the original subject. "So, what do *you* think about what Kate said?"

"I think it's fantastic," Dad flashed me a grin, "but it's going to mean an incredible amount of discipline and hard work from you, not to mention money. Ice and coaching time don't come cheap. Mom and I will support you one hundred per cent if this is what you want to do. Kate told me that potentially, you have what it takes to go to the top. And she knows."

That really scared me. Kate really did know. She'd skated competitively fifteen years ago, and had been coaching ever since. In the last five years, Kate had become one of the most respected coaches in Canada, even in North America. Suddenly things seemed to be moving a little too fast. Half an hour ago, I had been a regular competitive skater, with the same dreams that most skaters have: to work hard, skate in international competitions, and maybe someday go to the Olympics or turn professional. But everyone knows that very few make it to the top, that a lot of skaters are destined to skate either for fun or for bit parts in ice shows. That doesn't stop anyone from dreaming, of course, and it certainly didn't stop me.

"But I'm only twelve," I blurted. I thought I had a long way to go before I would be faced with this kind of opportunity.

"Twelve isn't too young, Jennie. You know that. Look at Tara Lipinski. She was world champion at fourteen."

"I know."

"Skating has been your whole life, Jennie. Is this what you want?"

"Of course," I answered. Of course it was. Kate's words were the ones I had been waiting to hear since I began skating when I was six.

Dad thumped the steering wheel in excitement. "Then let's do it!" he said exuberantly. "I'm so proud of you, Jen. Wait until we tell Mom!"

I sank back into the car seat, confused by the mix of emotions churning inside me. "Yeah," I said weakly. "I can't wait."

2 Making It Happen

"Height, Jennie! Put some oomph into it!" Kate hollered from the side of the rink.

It was five forty-five in the morning, and I felt especially sluggish. Kind of weird, when you think I should have been riding high on Kate's comments from the night before. Dad had been excited and talkative all evening, and Mom's eyes glowed with pride when I told her what my coach had said. My whole family seemed to think this was terrific news. Even my seven-year-old brother, Dylan, who isn't impressed by anything, told me that if I became famous, he would stop tying my skate laces in never-ending knots whenever we had a fight.

"Come on, Jen. Snap out of it. We've got work to do." Kate called.

We were working on my double loop. I had landed it a few months ago, but it wasn't as stable as it should be. Kate wanted to work on my technique before we began pushing toward landing a double Axel.

"Once more. And this time, *jump!*" Kate called.

I lifted my chin, extended my arms and began my approach to the jump. I could hear my skate blades whirring against the ice; the cool air rushed past my cheeks. I tried to relax, concentrating on timing the takeoff.

I launched myself into the air. Once, twice around. Everything seemed to move in slow motion. I touched down smoothly on my right skate. I turned to find Kate staring at me, lost in thought. "Well?" I asked.

"Geez, Jennie," she said. "You make it look so easy. You look like you're floating." Kate shook her head, as though to clear her thoughts. "Okay," she barked. "Extend that back leg a little more on the landing. And focus on your arms as you pull out of the revolutions. They shouldn't flap. Try and keep your elbows a little higher and stretch, okay? Try it again."

I blinked. I was used to the corrections. I wasn't used to Kate looking at me like I'd performed a minor miracle.

"Come on, Jennie. I don't have all day."

I grinned. *That* was the Kate I knew. I prepared for the jump and threw myself into the air again. This time I couldn't quite complete both revolutions, missed my footing and landed with a thump on my rear end.

"Jennie! What was that? Try it again," Kate bellowed.

I scrambled up and brushed the ice shavings off my leggings. This time I took a deep breath and visualized my approach to the jump. "You can do this," I told myself. "Just concentrate." I circled the rink, building up speed. As I neared Kate's position by the boards, I mohawked, positioned my skates and thrust my body upwards. This time I felt tighter, more in control, and the two revolutions were easy. I landed cleanly.

"Good girl!" Kate shouted.

My ribs heaved as I skidded to a stop. Jumping takes a lot of energy, and I didn't feel like I had any this morning. I couldn't forget that half the world was still asleep, while I was in this chilly rink trying to defy gravity.

Kate waved me over to her. "That was much better. Very clean. That's the kind of technique I want to see. Now, remember how that felt, okay? Remember it, because I'll want to see it again this afternoon."

I groaned.

"I know it's tough, but I want to start working on your double Axel again. You've got to nail it before Sectionals."

"Yeah. I know," I said.

"I also think we should start an extra weight training session for you. Start building that leg strength a little more. The jumps will come easier if you can get more height."

I groaned again.

Kate gave me a friendly shove. "What kind of championship attitude is that?" she said.

"Not a good one," I joked.

"That's for sure. Meet me in the weight room twenty minutes before practice this afternoon, okay? We'll start working out a new training program."

"Okay."

"You have almost half an hour before practice is over," Kate said, "and I have a lesson with Nicole and Brad now, so do some stretching and cool off a bit. Maybe work on some spins and footwork. And your spiral. I want to see it a lot steadier."

"Okay," I repeated. I found a bare patch of ice and practised a few waltz jumps and then moved into a flying camel. I studied the marks my blades made in the ice. You can tell if a spin isn't centred by the marks the blades make in the ice. Mine had wandered a little bit, but weren't too bad.

"You travelled way too far on that spin."

I looked up to see Amy Sehlmeier leaning over the boards at the edge of the rink.

"Hi, Amy," I said without enthusiasm.

"I'm surprised Kate was so easy on you this morning. Your double loop looked awfully sloppy."

My temper flared, but I bit the inside of my cheek and said nothing. I knew Amy was baiting me.

Amy and I used to be close friends until a few

months ago. During the summer, when we were at skating camp, she acted kind of weird — distant, and very critical of both her skating and mine. Then, when we started grade seven this fall, she started hanging out with different kids at school and somehow decided I was totally uncool. I don't know why, exactly. I mean, I'm not a major geek or anything.

I am kind of quiet, though. I really don't like to be the centre of attention, except when I'm skating. Then I can concentrate so hard that I forget that the audience and the judges are watching me.

But at school, I'm scared to be in the spotlight. It's easier to be ignored than to be picked on for being nerdy. Unless you know what kinds of things are cool to say, it's better to say nothing at all. Otherwise, some bozo is sure to start kidding around and embarrass the heck out of you. I'm never really quite sure what is cool and what isn't, so mostly I keep my mouth shut. Amy is just the opposite. She loves to be noticed, and is always doing something to get everyone's attention. She *definitely* knows how to be cool.

"Jennie! Hello? I'm talking to you!" Amy said. "You have to get it together on that spin, or the judges are going to slaughter you at Sectionals. You have the beginning okay," she said, demonstrating the approach to the jump. "But you have to use more control in the spin."

"Amy, I'd like to get some work done, if you don't mind."

"Of course!" Amy feigned politeness. "That's why I'm trying to help."

"Well, thanks, but that's okay. I'll just work on it myself."

"Okay, if you say so." Amy gave me a look I couldn't read. "I'll see you at school, then."

I glided backwards as Amy skated off the ice. I knew I'd be late, but I didn't feel like sharing the locker room with Amy, and I wanted to prove to myself that I could do a flying camel that was better than my first one. And — if the truth were told — better than what Amy could do.

I concentrated hard as I began a series of back crossovers. I didn't need too much speed for this flying spin, but I wanted to get enough momentum to make it spectacular. I jumped and swung into the spin. As I made the ninth revolution and began to pull up, I lowered my back leg and tightened my body so the speed of the spin increased. I finished with a blurring scratch spin. When I stopped, I looked down at the ice. The spin was nicely centred, tight and clean.

So there, Amy.

I glided to the boards and retrieved the sweatshirt that I kept in my skate bag. Tugging it over my head, I began to stroke around the outside of the rink. I felt my muscles relax as I pulled the scrunchie out of my ponytail and let the cool air swirl through my hair. Most of the other skaters had gone; the rink was nearly empty.

I found myself wondering about Amy for the hundredth time. It was becoming hard to realize that she had once been my best friend. She used to be fun to hang out with. We used to go to the snack bar by the public rink for frozen yogurt, and groan and gossip about practice.

Sometimes we'd sleep over at each other's houses and go to practice together on Saturday mornings. We did homework together in front of the TV — at least we did at her house, my parents never let me do that — we pigged out on ice cream and pizza, and watched movies and told each other secrets. When we were eight, we pretended we were skating in the Olympics, using my basement floor as a make-believe ice rink. We would glide and twirl on slippery sock-feet, and pretend to accept the gold medal. In those days, there were enough gold medals to go around.

She was the only friend who understood how important figure skating was to me, because she felt exactly the same way. But over the summer Amy changed. We had always competed against each other, but suddenly *everything* became a competition.

I'm not saying I'm not competitive, too. I am, of course. I wouldn't have stuck with skating this long if I wasn't. I just don't think that you have to hate your competition to be the best.

But I'm beginning to think that Amy does.

3 The Royal Family

Mom? Can you just let me off here, please?" I unfas-
tened my seat belt and grabbed my knapsack and the
strap of my skate bag.

Mom stared at me. She was driving to work, and
dropping me off at school on the way from morning
practice. Her short dark hair was sleek, her navy wool
suit tailored and professional. She exuded efficiency,
and it was hard to argue with her. "Honey, we're still
three blocks from school, and it's snowing."

"Mom, please? Okay? It's no big deal. I don't mind
the snow."

She looked at me like I had gone insane. "You just
spent twenty minutes complaining after practice about
how cold your feet were, and now you don't mind
walking in the snow in those?" She glanced down at
the navy tennis sneakers that I wore. Snow boots were
not cool.

"Mom, you don't understand. Kids who get

dropped off at the front of the school by their mothers look like total geeks. Everyone stares at you, unless you have a bunch of friends with you."

Mom rolled her eyes. "Oh, for pete's sake, Jennie …"

"Mom, come on." My fingers twitched on the door handle. We were almost at the junior high school.

Mom pulled the car over to the curb. "I could drive around through the back way, and drop you off at the loading docks for the cafeteria, if you really want to be inconspicuous," she said.

"Ha, ha. Very funny." I leaned over and kissed her cheek quickly. "Thanks."

"See you tonight," she called, as I slammed the car door shut. I walked briskly along the sidewalk toward the school. The snow fell thickly in wet, clumpy flakes that melted as soon as they hit the sidewalk. In a matter of seconds my shoes were soaked. I hurried up the steps at the side of the school and walked around to the front, where most of the seventh graders hung out. Groups of kids huddled near the doors, waiting for the bell.

In spite of my wet sneakers, I felt a sense of relief that I could blend in unnoticed. That's one of the weirdest things about junior high. Suddenly everything you do is either cool or uncool, and if you know what's good for you, you'll never, ever be uncool. It's a social death sentence. Adults — parents especially —

just don't understand this. My mom, for instance, finds it hard to believe that I can skate in front of more than a hundred spectators, but am afraid of walking up to a group of ten kids at school. I can't explain it to her. It's just the way it is.

When I compete on the ice, I'm supposed to be performing, and I'm judged on how well I skate. At school, I'm judged by a whole different set of rules, and I haven't figured them all out yet.

"Hi, Jennie." Amy was standing with Kallana Ohlmstead and a group of girls from our class.

"Hi," I said briefly and sidled past. I knew it was not an invitation to stop by the tone of Amy's voice. It was show-offy, with an edge of pity, as though I was so alone I needed someone to be kind.

There are only a few things I really hate about this school: dissecting earthworms, wearing the world's ugliest gym shorts, the lunchroom — which smells like moldy old tuna fish — and popularity politics.

Suddenly, belonging to a group of friends — the right group — is the single most important reason for existence at Meadowpark Junior High. And Amy, with her cute, petite, blonde prettiness, was right in the thick of things.

She leaned over and whispered something to Kallana, who laughed an airy, confident laugh designed to make the other girls in the group look up to see what they were missing. She leaned back against the iron railing on the stairs and surveyed the groups of kids on the front lawn, as though she were looking over her own private kingdom. And in a way, she was. Kallana was ultra-cool. To be included in Kallana's group was like being granted a temporary royal title.

I crouched miserably against the cold brick wall of the school. It's not like I don't have other friends besides Amy, who no longer really counted as a friend. I do, in fact, but I'm no popularity princess like Kallana. Because I'm always at the rink practising, I never have a chance to invite anyone over after school or on Saturday afternoons. So I hang out with certain kids at school, and we're friendly, but I don't really have a best friend. At least not anymore, I thought, looking at Amy.

Amy caught me looking and deliberately turned away. I wondered for what seemed like the millionth time what I had done to make her so angry that she not only would refuse to be friends, but also would try to make me feel left out on purpose. Because I knew very well that if Amy wanted to, she could have helped me make more friends at school — the right friends.

I am not a geek, I told myself. I am not. I am a nice person. Besides, no one who skates as well as I can could be a real geek, could they? Maybe they could. I wasn't sure what classified someone as a geek. I was pretty sure I wasn't ugly. I might not be small with long blond hair and a pixie face like Amy, but I don't think I'm ugly. Just kind of average, I guess.

My hair is thick and dark, and reaches past my shoulders in a tangled mass of natural curls. My eyes are a light, clear blue. Those are the good things. The bad things are that my skin is becoming a problem, but so far, if I scrub my face with medicated soap every night, I don't get too many zits. I'm also tall, which makes me feel like a clod next to tiny girls like Amy. *And* I have to wear braces on my teeth for at least the next four years.

Geez, I sound like I'm obsessed with my face. I think it's horrible, the way everyone believes that how you look is so important. But the fact is, some things are easier if you're beautiful, and it seems that being popular is one of them. I watched Amy giggling with the other girls. Amy was definitely the prettiest. I was sure that had something to do with why those girls wanted her for a friend, because there was no way she had any more time after school or on weekends than I did. She was always at the rink with me.

"Watching the royal family?" Jane Evans whispered in my ear.

"Huh? Oh yeah," I said, startled. "I was just thinking."

Jane was the epitome of everything I'd just been thinking about. She was a nice person, very smart, had lots of interesting hobbies and I'd known her since grade four. But she was also a flat-chested tomboy — flatter even than me — and wore a variety of sports clothing handed down from her older brother. Grubby sweatpants were not considered cool, and since Jane never wore anything else, she was largely ignored by Kallana's group.

Jane glanced in their direction. "She isn't that much of a big deal, really."

"I know." I looked at the group and studied her. Kallana was tall, with pale blond hair cut in a short, blunt cut just under her ears. She wasn't pretty, which made her an exception to my theory about beauty and popularity going hand-in-hand. Her face was blunt featured, with small, narrow gray eyes, and a thin-lipped, waspish smile. But she made you think she was attractive, maybe because her clothes were all expensive and creatively designed — the kind every teenage girl would die to own. In a school where faded jeans, name-brand shirts and casual jackets were the norm, Kallana stood out as a kind of fashion icon. Today she wore a red plaid tam with black velvet trim pulled down, so only the tips of her blond hair stuck out like a fringe. Her black wool coat was unbuttoned, revealing a dark green rayon jersey — the stretchy, clingy kind — over a plaid mini-skirt that matched the tam. Black tights and clunky black oxfords completed her outfit.

When I describe it, it sounds ordinary enough, but it's the way she wore it, as though it didn't matter that the whole outfit must have cost around three hundred dollars at some trendy shop. She made it seem as though she just didn't care. Maybe that's what made her cool. If I wore a three hundred dollar outfit to school, I'd be petrified that it would somehow get wrecked. Kallana would wear hers to gym class if she was allowed.

The bell blasted across the school yard, and there was the usual crowded throng in the hallway.

"C'mon, I'll walk you to your locker," Jane said, and I was grateful for the company. There's something eerie about feeling alone in a crowd of hundreds.

4 Jennie Skates

I plunked my skate bag down on one of the benches in the locker room at the rink and kicked off my sneakers. I stripped off my socks, and pulled on a pair of thermal ones I use for skating. It felt good to pull them on over my cold toes.

I sighed as I sat down. For the past week, Amy had pretty much ignored me at school, and of course Kallana and the other girls in her group did the same. It made me feel like an insignificant bug — kind of a nuisance and not worth noticing unless it lands right on your nose.

Kate poked her head around the row of lockers. "Come on, Jennie! I have some extra ice time booked for the club. Let's get out there!"

"Okay!" I called. "I'll be right there." Time to forget about friends and school. I smiled in relief and hurriedly tore off my jeans and pulled on a pair of black leggings. I tugged a sweatshirt over my T-shirt and grabbed my thermal gloves. I knew I'd be practising jumps today, and for skaters, falling goes with jumping. The gloves would help protect my hands from the ice.

I jammed everything into my locker and slammed the door shut. Picking up my skates, I hurried out to the rink. I knew Kate would be waiting impatiently, but I also knew better than to step out onto the ice without warming up and stretching first. Kate had lectured me at least a million times about how important it was to warm up before skating. It's very easy to pull a muscle or get injured if you don't, and injuries can take months to heal.

I propped one leg up on the ballet barre that the skating club had fastened to the wall nearest the locker rooms. I stretched carefully, trying to be thorough and hurry at the same time. Ice time is expensive, and you don't waste it if you can help it. After rushing through my warmup exercises, I laced my skates and slipped off the plastic guards.

Kate was correcting Nicole Alston and Brad Komanchuk on a star lift. They were pairs skaters who were also at the novice level. Nicole and I were friends, but she spent so much time working with Brad that last year we — that is, Amy and I — called them the Inseparable Two.

"Nicole, you have to really use your legs. You have to help Brad get the momentum he needs to make the lift look effortless," Kate said.

Nicole frowned in concentration. "I'm not sure exactly how to do it without jumping."

"Don't jump. That will make the lift look jerky, and it will make it hard for Brad to maintain his balance. Bend your knees and push off the ice as you begin the lift. Try it again, maybe you'll be able to feel the difference."

"Didja get that, Ick?" Brad teased. "Do it right this time, okay?"

"Shut up, Brad. And don't call me that dumb name." Nicole grimaced as she whacked him on the shoulder.

"Ready to go, Jennie?" Kate said as Nicole and Brad moved off down the ice to practise the lift. Nicole waved at me, but I understood why she didn't stop to say hi. As I said before, serious skaters don't waste ice time. There's plenty of time for talking after practice. And Nicole and Brad were serious — as serious as I am.

"Ready as I'll ever be," I said, pulling on my gloves.

"All right, Jen. It's time to get to work. I mean, really work. You know what I told your Dad last week. Now it's time to put that talk into action. You sure you're ready for it?"

I felt a twinge of apprehension, but I swallowed it quickly. "Of course," I said.

"Okay. I want to work on your double Axel and the double toe-double loop combo today."

I gulped. "But I've never landed the double Axel."

"All the more reason we should start working on it, right?" Kate said.

I nodded.

"Your Axel is one of your strongest jumps. I think the double will be an easy progression for you. And of course, we have to nail a double Axel sometime, preferably for Sectionals."

I nodded again.

"Try a few jumps after you warm up and get the feel of the ice. Then we'll try the Axel."

"Okay." I circled the rink a few times and as I approached Kate again, I began to prepare for a double Salchow. Skating backwards, I executed a forward outside turn to the back inside edge of my right skate. I won't describe all the different edges but it's important to know that using the different edges of the skate blade are what gives a skater the ability to spin and jump smoothly.

As I built up power, I swung my free leg around and pushed off hard with my skating leg. I spun tightly in the air and landed cleanly on one foot. I skated toward Kate.

"Good. Watch your free leg. Don't let it whip around your skating leg. It'll throw off your position. Do it again."

I flew into another Salchow, and landed easily.

"Okay." Kate waved me over. "Let's try the Axel. I want you to slow down your position just before the takeoff. Wait until the very last moment to thrust up and lift off the ice. All right?"

I took a deep breath. "Okay." I moved off to start the approach for the jump. I knew I had to get even more power and momentum to complete the two and a half rotations in the air, so I swept across the ice with as much speed as I could.

I counted in my head, carefully timing the takeoff. Ready ... push! I thought. I launched myself upward and flung myself into the turns. I managed one and a half — only enough for a single Axel — before I thudded onto the ice on my backside.

"Not bad," Kate said as I scrambled up. "Try again and make sure your free leg and your arms are moving at exactly the same time to create the lift."

I did the jump again. And again. And again. I groaned and rubbed my hip as I hit the ice for the fourth time. "Kate, my butt is killing me. I can't even manage to two-foot the landings. I'm totally out of control."

"I know it's tough," Kate agreed. "You have to get so much more speed and momentum that when you hit, you hit hard." She grinned. "Just wait until we try triples!"

I grimaced.

"Don't worry," Kate said. "It'll get easier."

"In the meantime," I grumbled. "I'll be black and blue all over."

"That's the price of skating," Kate answered cheerfully.

"Can't I use the harness?" I asked. The harness is what we call the mechanism that helps a skater learn jumps. It operates by hooking a belt around your waist and having someone tug on the pulley rope just as you jump. It creates a few extra seconds of lift, so you can learn the correct positions for a jump without always crashing to the ice.

"Maybe tomorrow. But I want you to get the feel of it yourself, first."

I groaned again.

"One more time." Kate pointed down the rink. I did the jump again, and this time managed to get my feet underneath me to hold the landing, even though it was on two feet.

"See?" Kate gloated. "You almost made the two and a half rotations, and you didn't fall. You're improving already."

"Yeah, but it's a long way from perfect," I said glumly.

Kate shook her finger at me. "You'd think you didn't know that skating takes years of effort. It's a slow progression, remember?"

"I know, I know."

"Time's up, anyway. I have a lesson with Amy now. Work on the jump combination, instead. I want at least five repetitions, all of them 110 per cent effort. Okay?"

"Okay." I backed off to a corner of the ice and focused on the double toe-double loop combination.

It's difficult, and even though I can land it consistently, I still have to give it everything I've got to do a really good one. My shoulders felt tight and I stretched out before attempting the jumps.

I could see Kate talking to Amy. Amy was nodding enthusiastically, and then backed off to work on a sit-spin. As I watched I could see how technically, the spin was correct, but it lacked power. Amy didn't move into it gracefully, and she lacked the momentum to make the spin tight and fast. Kate appeared to agree with me, because from her gestures, I guessed she was telling Amy the same thing. Amy backed off to try the spin again, and when she noticed me watching, scowled in my direction. I turned away and began the first of my five combinations.

I nailed the first two, then had to try hard for the next three. I took a quick break after the fifth, and wiped the sweat from my forehead. It may seem odd to be boiling hot in an ice rink, but jumping over and over again is a heck of a workout.

"Hey, Jen. Nice jumping." Nicole glided by, a water bottle in one hand.

"Thanks. What are you and Brad working on?"

"Still that stupid star lift. Brad just can't hold me up long enough."

"Maybe you're too heavy," I teased. Nicole is only about four foot ten, and weighs about ninety pounds. Brad is almost six feet. I knew he had no trouble lifting her.

Nicole laughed. "I don't think that's the problem."

"Hey, you two!" Kate hollered down the ice. "Get back to work!"

"See ya!" Nicole skated away and I returned wearily to the combination jumps. By now I'd had enough. My feet were getting cold, my rear end was damp where the ice shavings had melted into my tights, and I was ready for a hot shower. My leg muscles ached. It was a relief when I finished the last jump. It was nearly five o'clock, and practice was over.

I opened the gate in the boards and dug my skate guards from under a bleacher. I was about to clunk my way into the locker room when Kyle Javer waved from the doorway to the pro shop.

Kyle's mom and my mom are friends, so we've known each other practically forever. He lives on my street and is in my class at school, he plays hockey at the rink, and his dad owns the pro shop, so he helps out there sometimes. We've always been buddies, but since Amy dumped me, we've hung out together a lot more. He's pretty much the closest friend I have, which may seem weird because he's a boy, but Kyle is funny and smart, and he couldn't care less about popularity. He thinks Kallana is a major snob.

"Hey, Jennie," he called. "Come over here for a second."

I climbed laboriously over the pile of skate bags on

the floor and clumped through the rink door. "What's up?"

"Guess what I have?" he said.

I shrugged. "Beats me."

"Something you'd be *very* interested in."

"So tell me."

"Don't you want to know?" he grinned mischievously.

I smiled. "Maybe. I'll tell you when I know what it is."

"You know how my mom gets all those free tickets?" Kyle said.

"Yeah," I said impatiently. Mrs. Javer works for a local public relations agency. She receives tickets to all kinds of events — movies, concerts, you name it — for publicity give-aways, and she often brings home any tickets that are left over.

"My mom just got five tickets to see Elvis Stojko. She said I could bring a friend, and I knew you'd kill me if I didn't ask you. You want to go?"

I let out a screech. "Really? Sure!" I said eagerly. Elvis was an absolutely terrific skater. He'd won the world figure skating championships three times. I really loved watching top skaters. Television was fine, but live was the best.

"Are you going to go?"

"Well, sure. It's not hockey, but I'll bring a comic book for the boring parts."

I pounded him on the shoulder. "Figure skating is not boring!"

Kyle laughed. "Okay, okay." He grabbed my fist. "It's the most fascinating sport I've ever seen."

"Liar." I gave him a mock glare. "When is it?"

"In three weeks, on a Saturday afternoon. Can you get out of practice?"

I hesitated. "I don't know. I'll have to check. Maybe Kate will let me off, just this once."

"Okay … well, I'll see you at school."

"Okay. And Kyle … thanks!" He grinned as I clunked back down the hall toward the ladies' locker room. I smiled to myself as I began to unlace my skates. Kyle was really nice, I thought. And it would be so great to see Elvis skate. Maybe I could even get his autograph after the show.

Amy walked by and opened the door of her locker. "I saw you and Kyle talking," she said.

"Umm-hmm," I answered. I concentrated on pulling the guards off my skates and carefully wiping the blades dry with a rag. I'd forgotten to do it when I came off the ice, and it's important, so that the blades don't rust.

"He's totally cute," Amy persisted.

I felt myself stiffen. She knew Kyle and I were friends — we'd practically grown up together, for pete's sake.

"Umm-hmm." I said, tucking the damp rag back into my skate bag.

Amy fixed me with a blank stare. "So is this some big romance?" she said.

I looked up, annoyed. "No, of course not." I said flatly. Amy silently gathered up her things. I pulled on my jeans. When she had left, I pulled a hairbrush out of my bag and yanked the scrunchie out of my ponytail and began to comb my hair. The stiff bristles of the brush felt good against my sweaty scalp. I brushed harder.

I'm almost positive Amy likes Kyle. Why else would she ask me nosy questions about him? And she always giggles when he's around. It hurt that she was keeping secrets from me. We used to tell each other everything. Before, Amy would have told me if she had a crush on Kyle. The way things had become between us, I could only guess how she felt, what she was thinking.

A raw soreness, like sandpaper on a sunburn, hurt deep inside my chest. What had I ever done to lose my best friend? And what was worse, I didn't trust her anymore. I found myself freezing up around her, especially when she kept making me feel like such an idiot.

I tossed my practice clothes into my skate bag and picked it up. The light, happy feeling I had after talking to Kyle was completely gone. Now all I could think of was skating, and how my competition with Amy seemed to extend far beyond the ice.

5 The Great Egg Incident

My eyelids felt sandy, and I stifled a yawn. It was Tuesday afternoon, midway into my first class after lunch — the worst time of the day. I was feeling the effects of early morning practice, a peanut butter sandwich and milk at noon, and Mrs. Kilton's soft, droning voice in social studies class. The room felt warm, and I was so drowsy I wanted to put my head down on my desk and have a nap.

Mrs. Kilton spoke in a normal voice most of the time, but during her lectures, she lapsed into a pleasant monotone that lulled her students into a kind of stupor. If she ever decided to quit teaching, I was sure she could make a fortune curing insomniacs. I wasn't the only one in class who had a hard time paying attention, and with the extra effort I'd been putting in at practice, I was definitely the most likely to conk off.

Propping my chin in my hand, I glanced around the classroom. Kyle was reading a hockey magazine under his desk, Amy was doodling in the margin of her workbook, and Kallana was filing her nails behind her open textbook.

I found myself studying her. Kallana was by far the most noticeable person in the room. Today she had on a black rayon slip dress over a white T-shirt, compared to the jeans most of the kids wore. I remembered Amy telling me the first week of school that Kallana dressed and looked the way she did because Kallana's mother used to work as a fashion buyer for a big chain of department stores, and now runs her own modelling agency. Amy had been awed by that information, but at the time, all I could think of was how awful it would be to have a mother who thought that appearance was everything. No sweatshirts, no worn-out jeans, no T-shirts with holes in the armpits and pizza stains on the front. There was no question that it had rubbed off on Kallana. I think she'd rather die than wear a grubby, old, stained T-shirt.

Kallana must have felt my eyes on her, because she turned in her seat, raised her eyebrows and gave me a searching look. I let my gaze fall to my desk, and picked up my pencil.

"All right, everyone," Mrs. Kilton said. "Listen up!" Her voice had returned to normal, now that she'd finished a lengthy discussion about yesterday's exam. "Today's the day we start our group projects." She flashed us a smile, but there was steel behind it, and I dreaded the next words. I knew she wouldn't stand for any whining about the groups we were about to be assigned. Mrs. Kilton is big on fairness, and tells us constantly that it's important to learn to work with everybody, not just your friends.

"I've divided the class into five groups, and you'll be working within these groups for the next three weeks."

I hoped I'd get a nice, easy-going group. Maybe if I was really lucky I'd get to work with Kyle. That would make things a lot easier. I held my breath as Mrs. Kilton read off the names for the first two groups. Then she started on the next one.

"Tim, Jennie, Kallana, Jaspal and Amy will be group three ..."

My breath exhaled in a soft hiss. Kallana? *And* Amy? Was Mrs. Kilton deliberately trying to make me miserable? How could she do this to me? And I had to try and work with them on the same project for *three whole weeks*?

I suppressed a shudder. I had seen Kallana make life difficult for several kids, the type who were obviously different. One poor guy had two front teeth that were so badly bucked, Kallana nicknamed him The Beav, and constantly asked him how the dam was coming along. An overweight girl whose name was Lydia Tubman was always referred to as Tubman, with a marked emphasis on the first syllable. The examples could go on forever.

Mrs. Kilton handed out copies of a thick booklet on the project. The title was printed on the cover: It said "Marooned" in big letters. As the five of us pushed our desks together to form a make-shift table, Tim Dupries accidently hit his workbook with his elbow and sent it flying onto the floor. I winced on his behalf. Tim was skinny, extremely self-conscious, with a thin, chirpy voice and a pimple-blotched face — definitely someone Kallana would enjoy making fun of.

Tim's face reddened; he scooped the book off the floor, not caring if he crumpled the pages in his haste. Before Kallana could made a remark, I spoke up.

"So, this looks kind of interesting, don't you think?" I addressed Jaspal Singh, because his was by far the friendliest face in the group.

"Uh … yes. I guess so," he said, giving me a small smile. He darted a look at Kallana, who made an effort to look extremely bored.

"Looks like a big yawn to me," she said.

Amy quickly adjusted her facial expression to match Kallana's. "Yeah, no kidding," she said.

Embarrassed, I opened the first page of the booklet and pretended to read. I'd been hoping for more backup from Jas, who is both smart and easy-going, but he never says much. I think it's because, even though he can speak English well, he doesn't feel very confident talking to the other kids. His family had moved from India to Canada only last year.

Mrs. Kilton stood at the front of the room and waited for everyone to settle down. "Listen please," she said. "We won't begin working with the booklets until next time, so you can put them away. Today we're going to do an exercise on creativity and cooperation, to teach us something about working as a team." She smiled. "This is going to be fun."

Kallana snorted under her breath.

"Here are the rules. Each team gets an egg. I will mark off a length at the front of the room for a race track. I want you to think of as many ways to transport your egg through the race as possible, without using your hands, or touching it with more than one body part. Once one body part has touched the egg, you can't use it again. Methods of transporting the egg can only be used once. You have to be fast, because once one team has decided on a method, no other team can use the same one. Don't let other teams overhear your discussions. All's fair in egg racing, after all!" Mrs. Kilton said brightly. "Are there any questions?"

"Who's the winner?" Amy asked.

"The winner is the team who completes the most races. Each race must use a different method, of course, so your creativity had better be flowing!" Mrs. Kilton raised a finger. "One more thing: If you break your egg, your team is automatically disqualified. It's also up to you whether you want one person to do all the races, or whether each teammate will take a turn." She looked around the room. "All right? Any other questions?"

There weren't. I had been scribbling busily in my binder, but glanced up as Mrs. Kilton placed an egg on Tim's desk. It swayed gently in its ceramic bowl.

"All right. Everyone get started. You have ten minutes to discuss racing methods before we begin."

Tim, Jas and I looked at each other apprehensively, wondering who would have the guts to speak up first. Kallana frowned. "This is a total waste of time," she said. "If my mom knew what kind of junk they taught us in this school, she'd put me in WIC right this second."

"WIC?" Amy said.

"West Island College. It's a private school." Kallana answered.

"Yeah, but then you'd actually have to do some work," I said, before my brain registered what I'd just said.

Kallana's eyes hardened. "Oh yeah?"

Mrs. Kilton clapped her hands. "People! Only five minutes left!"

"Uh, okay," Tim said nervously, intercepting the frigid look Kallana shot at me. "We could push the egg along the floor with our noses."

"That'll only work for one race." Amy said.

"One race is better than none," I said. "Amy could drag the egg along the floor on top of her hair," I suggested, eyeing Amy's long, thick waves. "Probably no one else would use that method."

"Oh, that's disgusting, Jennie. I'm not getting my hair all gross." Amy pretended to gag.

"You got a better idea, then?" I said.

"We could kick it," Amy said.

"Too easy for it to break," said Jaspal, shaking his head. "We'd be disqualified."

"Two minutes until race time, folks!" Mrs. Kilton called.

"Listen you guys," I said. "We have to make some decisions. Amy, use your hair, and forget about it getting messed up, unless you can come up with some brainstorm first. Tim, do your nose. That's the most obvious idea, so you go first, and make sure you beat everyone else to it. Jas, use your feet somehow without kicking it, and Kallana ..." I swallowed as she glared at me. "... use your elbows. I'll use my chin. If we make it through all five races, we'll have to come up with some other ideas. Okay?"

"Who appointed you boss?" Kallana said, crossing her arms over her chest.

I might ask you the same question, I thought, but I didn't say anything. Tight-lipped, I began to jot down the racing ideas.

"I think Jennie's right," Tim said timidly.

"Nobody asked you," Kallana muttered.

"All right, people. Let's get started." Mrs. Kilton

46

clapped her hands. "First racers from each team come to the front of the room."

Tim stepped up nervously and joined the students from the other teams.

"Place your eggs on the floor in front of you. Hands behind your backs." said Mrs. Kilton. "Nobody move until I say go. Remember, if someone else uses your racing method first, you have to think of something else. Okay? Ready ... and ... GO!"

Tim, true to my instructions, threw himself flat on the floor in his eagerness to be the first nose-pusher in the race. Unfortunately his vehemence sent his egg rolling forward, out of reach of his face. By the time he had wriggled forward, Jill Matlow had already connected her nose to her egg.

"Quick, Tim. Do something else!" I cried frantically. The rest of the class was cheering as their teammates nudged their eggs along. One used his forehead, another a shoulder, a third was using her left ear. Tim lay on the floor with a stunned expression on his face.

I forgot all about acting cool. "Tim, come on! Do your chin! Use your chin!" I screeched. Amy was shouting, too, until Kallana snickered, then she shut up. Jaspal stood behind me, watching silently. Tim lifted his face, nudged the egg with his chin and scrunched his body forward. It took a only a few seconds for him to catch up to the other teams. Rolling the egg forward with every explosive jut of his chin, Tim eased it over the finish line.

"Quick, Jas. You go next. I have to think of a different way to race." Jaspal nodded and positioned himself behind the egg, gently pushing it forward with one foot. Then he hopped a few paces on the other leg and nudged the egg yet again. It was a good start, because two other kids were bickering over who was the first one to begin shoving an egg with their right ear, and it was causing a lot of confusion. But good old Jas kept going. He was first through the finish line.

"Amy, go next," I said. I still hadn't thought of a new way to race the egg.

"No way!" Amy said. "I'm going last."

"I'm not going at all," Kallana said. "I'm not going to look stupid, crawling around on the floor." It was on the tip of my tongue to protest that Mrs. Kilton said she had to do it, but I could just hear Kallana mimicking, "Mrs. Kilton says! Mrs. Kilton says! What are you, teacher's pet or something?" I decided to keep my mouth shut.

"Okay, I'll go, then." I had no idea what I would do. I kept trying to remember all the body parts that had already been used. The only thing I could think of was sliding sideways and using one hip. So that's what I did. It looked ridiculous, bumping the egg with the side of my bum, then wriggling crab-like a few inches further along the floor. I could hear Amy and Kallana giggling hysterically and I gritted my teeth.

I gave the egg a hard shove, then lifted my rear end scuttled sideways on my elbows and feet. As I tried to peer over my stomach, looking for the egg, I felt my elbow skid, and I lost my balance. My backside came down with a thump. There was a soft crunch, then I felt sloppy goo spread underneath my jeans. I winced and my face turned hot.

Amy and Kallana doubled over, snorting with laughter. Jaspal leaned over and helped me to my feet. Even Mrs. Kilton wasn't sure what to say, but Tim found the words.

"I guess this means we're disqualified."

6 Double Trouble

I laced my skates angrily, stood up and tugged at the skirt of my purple skating dress. I don't normally bother wearing a dress to practice, but after the egg fiasco at school, I felt like I needed any lift I could get. I was lucky that I usually packed at least two changes of practice clothes in my skate bag, because I would have to wear my black skating leggings home, since my jeans were an absolute wreck.

I surveyed myself in the locker room mirror. The dress flowed softly over my hips, and for once I'd managed to secure my curls into a smooth bun at the back of my head. I felt almost like a professional skater. There was absolutely nothing about my appearance for Amy to make fun of, and I was determined that there would be nothing in my skating performance for her to find fault with either. With that thought in mind, I marched out on the ice.

Kate was drilling Nicole and Brad on footwork, so

I began my warm-up by stroking around the rink. Soon the fresh, cool air began to make me feel better, and my muscles gradually loosened up. It felt good to work off some of the frustration and humiliation of the day, and very soon I felt ready to try some jumps.

I decided to start with the double Axel. I positioned myself carefully, and after making sure there were no other skaters nearby, I launched into the jump. Once! Twice! I spun in the air. I felt like I was floating. Then my skate touched down, and even though I wobbled, I actually held the landing. I stopped abruptly, so shocked that I nearly lost my balance and fell. I had landed it! My first double Axel! I felt like throwing my hands up in the air and cheering, but instead I looked to see if Kate had noticed. She hadn't. She was deep in conversation with Josh, demonstrating his arm position to hold Nicole in the lift.

But someone else had. Amy was staring across the ice at me with undisguised envy. I had to smother a smile of satisfaction. Well, Amy, I thought, you might be able to make me feel like a complete moron at school, but I can compete here. At least on the ice I know what I'm doing.

My satisfaction died when I made a second attempt at the jump. I threw myself into it, hoping for the same lift, the same floating feeling as before, but instead I felt heavy and slow. I came down hard on two feet, barely completing two revolutions.

"Height, Jennie! And let's focus on some control," Kate hollered, skating over.

Typical, I thought, that Kate would see the horrible jump and miss the good one.

"But Kate, I landed it!" I protested. "I actually did, just a few minutes ago. It wasn't great, but I hung on to the landing."

"Really?" Kate pursed her lips thoughtfully. "That's pretty good. Quite an improvement, then."

"Yeah." I looked at her.

"Well, what are you waiting for?" Kate said. "Let's see it again! And this time do it right."

I backed up for another attempt. Out of the corner of my eye, I could see Amy watching. It made me feel a little more nervous, but I was determined to do it.

Even though I used all my strength to push myself into the air, I had my position wrong. My body twisted on the second revolution, and I fell to the ice with a thump.

Kate shook her head. "Keep trying!" she yelled, turning back to Nicole and Brad.

I stood up painfully and brushed the ice shavings from my legs. Then I took a deep breath. All right, Jennie, I told myself, concentrate! You can do this. I stroked slowly around the rink, gradually building up speed. I was flying by the time I reached the far end of the ice again, and threw myself once more into the jump.

Again, I could feel that my timing was off, and I crashed to the ice. As I spun to a stop on my rear end, I wondered if I should try a more careful approach. I felt Amy watching me as I tried edging gingerly into the jump, instead of vaulting into it with total abandon. That didn't work either. I only managed one rotation, before both feet connected with the ice.

"Darn!" I slapped my thigh in exasperation. "I've been working on this move forever. Why can't I land it more than once?" I muttered.

I decided to go through my warm-up again. Maybe stretching out would make me feel less tense. I glided to the gate in the boards and slipped on my skate guards. I did a few leg exercises, gently tugging at my hamstrings and lower back muscles. A blur of electric blue suddenly flashed in front of me. It was Amy, in a brand-new unitard, executing a brilliantly perfect flying camel. I chewed on my lip and turned away as irritation swelled in my chest. Amy was deliberately showing off. There was a whole expanse of fresh ice at the other side of the rink, but she had chosen to practise here, where I couldn't possibly miss seeing her. Especially after my last failed attempts to land that double Axel.

I'm not going to play games with you, Amy, I thought. I'm here to skate. I took a deep breath and stepped back out on the ice.

"Jen! Come on!" Kate hollered from the opposite end of the rink. "It's time for your lesson."

I hurried over. "Sorry, Kate. I just wanted to stretch out a little more."

"Ready to land that Axel again?" Kate said.

"Uh, well … I was working on it, but it doesn't seem to be getting any better."

"Try it again, Jennie. It's important for you to land this jump consistently before Sectionals, so let's get to work."

"Okay," I said.

"Remember to watch that free leg. It throws off your balance when you whip it around too fast."

I nodded. Once more I tried the jump, and once more I thumped on the ice.

Kate helped me up. "Jennie, your form is good. Great, even. I think you're trying too hard. You're tense when you take off, and it's ruining the whole thing."

I felt close to tears. "What can I do about it, then?"

"Let's run through your long program. If you have to single the double Axel, then do it, but give the double a try."

"All right." I skated to the middle of the rink and struck my opening pose. As the music blasted from the loudspeakers, I jumped and nearly missed my cue. But immediately Kate turned the volume to a normal level, and I started to skate.

I loved this routine. I felt so free, like a bird skimming over the ice. It was easy, smooth. Everything fit. The double Lutz; some footwork; a Beillmann spin, which requires a skater to grab the skate blade behind her back and stretch her leg upwards; a few field movements, and then into the double toe-double loop combination. I landed easily, and did some intricate footwork to the catchy rhythm of the song.

Next was the flying camel, and then the double Axel. I tried not to think. I let the music pull me along and lift me into the jump. Once more everything slowed down. I felt like I was floating, and caught my breath as I came down.

Only one skate touched the ice.

I wobbled; it wasn't perfect, but I had done it. I looked at Kate and smiled.

7 An Extra Edge

Did you talk to Kate about getting out of practice to see the skating exhibition?" Kyle asked. "It's this Saturday, you know." My mom had dropped us off at the rink and we were waiting for both hockey and figure skating practice to start. We leaned against the lobby wall at the rink, sharing a bag of potato chips from the vending machine.

"Yeah, I know. I haven't asked yet," I crunched, gulped and swallowed. "I was sort of waiting to see if I could sweet-talk her at the last minute. It's not going to be easy. Sectionals is only a few weeks away."

"Well, you'd better hurry up. I might have to ask somebody else," Kyle said.

I eyed him, hurt. "Really?"

Kyle snorted and nearly choked on a potato chip. "No way! If you don't go, you think I'm going to sit through a figure skating exhibition with my mother and her friends? Get real! No, you owe me big time for this, Jennie. I'm only going because I know you really want to."

I smiled at him. "In that case, I'll bring extra potato chips, just for you."

"Better make 'em taco chips. I like those better." He grinned.

"Hey, Javer, get yer butt in here. Practice is starting." A hockey player dressed in goalie pads gestured at Kyle impatiently.

"I gotta go." Kyle crumpled the potato chip bag and tossed it into a nearby garbage can.

"See you after practice."

"Tell your mom not to wait for me. I'm helping my dad in the pro shop for a while tonight."

I nodded and picked up my skating stuff, waving a quick hello to Mr. Javer as I passed the pro shop. Kate was in the tiny office next door that she shared with the other figure skating coaches, the precision team coach, and the hockey coaches.

I swallowed uneasily. This was as good a time as any to ask her about skipping practice. Maybe if she hears it's to see Elvis Stojko skate, she'll think it's sort of educational, I reasoned. I hoped she would understand how much I was dying to see him. I knocked timidly on the open door.

"Kate?" I said when she looked up. "Do you have a minute?"

"Sure." Kate laid down the folder she was writing in. "What's up?"

I got right to the point. "I … um … was wondering if I could maybe … uh, miss practice on Saturday afternoon. It's really important."

"Why?"

Briefly, I contemplated lying. She couldn't possibly refuse if I told her I had to go to the doctor's for a test for an incurable disease, or something as equally life-threatening. I knew from the expression on Kate's face that she wasn't going to swallow taking time off skating to goof off for the afternoon, even if it was to watch a famous skater.

I told the truth.

Kate frowned. "Jennie, I can understand your wanting to go, but we only have two weeks left before Sectionals. Every second of practice time we have is essential, especially since we haven't nailed that double Axel yet."

"I've landed it twice," I said.

"I mean consistently. Jennie, I understand, I really do. But I'm afraid I have to say no, I don't think missing practice is a good idea right now. I'm sorry. Sometimes competing in the sport you love demands sacrifices, and this is one of them. Your social life has to be put on hold sometimes."

"Try *all* the time," I muttered.

"I know it seems rough, but you'll thank me when

you're on the medal podium in two weeks," Kate said, trying to grin.

Frustration tightened my chest, but I said nothing. After all, I had pretty much expected Kate's response. "Okay," I said. "I guess I'll go get ready for practice."

"See you on the ice," Kate answered.

I stomped toward the locker room without looking back.

★ ★ ★

Dad shoved a stack of old records away from the basement wall and handed me a dusty, dog-eared box. "Here, Jennie," he said. "Have a look through this."

I wrinkled my nose. "Yuck."

"Grime won't kill you," Dad replied. He grinned. "Especially if you want this exercise space."

"Mmm-hmm." I actually wasn't sure I wanted the exercise space. But Dad seemed to think that having a ballet barre and an open place to stretch at home would give me an extra edge. So, instead of spending Sunday afternoon — my only afternoon away from the rink — watching videos or just hanging out, I was helping my dad clean out the basement.

I heaved a sigh.

Dad must have sensed how I felt. "Don't worry, Jenzo. I'll let you off the hook soon. Just help me for an hour or so, and get some of this junk shovelled out of here. I can lay down the linoleum and put up the barre by myself."

I felt pretty guilty. He was doing all of this work just for me. I shook my head. "It's okay, Dad. I don't mind helping." I dug through the box and started to laugh. "Look, Dad!" I held up a skating costume. It was orange satin with a yellow skirt and short, flame-red streamers dangling from the hips and shoulders. "Do you remember?"

Dad pushed his glasses further up his nose. "Of course! You wore that when you were six. You skated to 'You Are My Sunshine.'"

I giggled. "I must have looked so silly."

"You were the cutest kid out there. Everyone thought you were terrific, even then."

"I think I fell down twice," I said.

"You were still terrific," Dad insisted.

I shoved the costume back in the box and pulled out several pairs of worn leggings. "Gross," I muttered. "Why didn't these get thrown out?" I tossed them toward the junk heap that was growing in the corner.

"We'd better get some garbage bags and start hauling stuff out of here," Dad said. "Once we get some space cleared, I can measure out the linoleum."

"Okay." I rifled through the rest of the box, but only found some T-shirts and some of Mom's old books. "Do you think she wants to keep these?" I asked, holding up a paperback.

Dad peered at the title. *99 Ways to Redecorate Your Bathroom*. He winked. "I don't know. Maybe we'd better keep it, it might come it handy some day."

I started to laugh. "Dad!"

"Well, it might. The toilet needs to be replaced. We'd certainly want it to match our tasteful decor."

I snorted. Our bathroom is about as tasteful as skunk cabbage. It's cluttered with Dylan's bath toys, mismatched towels, a toothpaste-blobbed, chipped green sink, and an awful, green-and-white counter top. It's horrible. I made a face, then looked again at the book jacket. "On second thought," I said, laying the book aside, "we will keep it. Redecorating the bathroom is a real possibility."

"Not for a long time, Sweetie. Redecorating will have to wait until you get that Olympic gold. Skating costs too much to leave us money for such pleasures."

"Oh, Dad." I felt suddenly mournful. They were doing so much for me. What if it didn't pay off? "Dad …" I hesitated. "if I don't get to the Olympics …"

"Honey, you can't think like that. Of course you'll make it. Kate says you've got the talent, and Mom and Dylan and I are all rooting for you. We'll do whatever we have to help you succeed. Like this, for instance."

He gestured with a screwdriver to the barre he was attaching to the wall by its brackets. "We know you can do it. But you have to stay positive, too, okay?"

"Yeah," I muttered. Dad wasn't even letting me finish. I wanted to tell him that I wasn't so sure skating in that level of competition was for me. But how could I say that now? Silently I began to stack the books in a clean cardboard box and then laid some old flower vases carefully on top. As I taped the box shut, I began to realize that I hadn't thought very much about what exactly I wanted to do with a skating career.

I mean, I've always loved performing on the ice. But I'd gone from taking Saturday morning lessons at the rec center, to joining a competitive club and dreaming about Olympic gold, without really thinking about what I want from skating. Do I *really* want to be an Olympic champion? I wondered.

When Kate told my father she thought that I had the talent to go all the way, I was thrilled. Who wouldn't be? It was like a dream coming true at last. But now, in a way, it seemed almost like a little girl's dream — like wanting to be a princess or a movie star. Did anyone ever stop to think what living those lives might really be like?

I chewed on my lip. Becoming a top figure skater was going to mean years of much more work, and harder work, on the ice. It would mean turning down invitations to parties and things I might really want to do — like watching Elvis Stojko skate. I was still bummed out about missing that yesterday.

It also would mean putting up with other skaters like Amy. The higher the level of competition, I reasoned, the tougher the attitudes of some of the competitors. Some of them could probably make Kallana look like a fairy godmother by comparison.

But I really loved skating. Maybe I could work toward being in ice shows, or join a precision team instead of doing ladies' singles. Even as I thought about it, I knew it wouldn't work. Ice shows mostly hire well-known skaters for their lead parts, and unless I wanted to get stuck playing tiny parts forever, I'd have to do well in amateur skating. And as much as I think precision skating would be fun and interesting, they don't work on jumps the way single skaters do. And jumping is one of the things I enjoy most about skating.

Slowly I uncapped a black felt marker and scribbled a label on the side of a storage box. I loved performing on the ice. But that didn't mean I had to be an Olympic champion.

Did it?

8 My Ex-Best Friend

All right, people!" Mrs. Kilton clapped her hands for attention. "Grab your books, we're going to spend the class in the library." She held up an index finger as everyone started to move. "I want you to sit with your groups and work on the next chapter in the booklet. Make use of the library materials for this — it's part of your group report and will be graded. So do a good job!" She stepped back and there was a rush for the door.

Her cry of "Quietly, everyone!" was drowned by the clattering shuffle in the hallway.

Kyle edged up beside me. "Good luck with the ice queen," he said.

"Which one?" I asked bitterly. This group project had been a nightmare for the last week and a half. Kallana's barbed comments, and Amy's too-obvious approval of them, were beginning to grate on my nerves. Why couldn't the two of them just keep their mouths shut?

Kyle squeezed my arm and gave me an encouraging grin. I smiled back and felt better — until I slid into the chair beside Amy in the library.

Amy's mouth twisted as she fought to keep from snickering. "Hi, Jennie. I like your jeans."

"Thanks." My mouth felt dry. What now?

"There's something stuck on your seat, though. Looks like eggshells," she added, bursting into fresh giggles. Kallana joined in. Tim and Jaspal looked uncomfortable.

I could feel a hot flush creeping up my face. "Subtle. Real subtle, Amy." The great egg incident was something I wanted to forget as quickly as possible. I opened my book. "We'd better get started. Has anyone read this stuff yet?" I hadn't found much time for homework lately.

"It's about finding food on our desert island. We're supposed to think of different ways to get it, and research how tribes in other countries get food," Jaspal said.

Kallana wrinkled her nose, but before she could say anything I flipped to the questions at the back of the chapter. "So I guess we have to work on these."

Tim gaped. "'Find at least three articles on a hunter/gatherer tribe in South America or Africa and discuss their methods. Apply what you have learned to your imaginary desert island situation.' Are they crazy? It'll take hours to do that, and that's only one question!"

"That's why," I said patiently, "this is a group project. We divide up the questions, and it won't take very long to do the whole thing."

"Well, I'm not doing that one," Tim said. "I'll take … um," he scanned the questions anxiously, "geez, aren't there any true or false in here?"

I couldn't help laughing. "I don't think so."

"Okay, I'll do this one. List ten probable foods that you could find on your desert island." Tim counted on his fingers. "Let's see. There'd be bananas, probably, and mangoes. Bugs. For sure there'd be bugs, and you can eat those if you get really desperate …"

"Ugh." Amy made a face like she was throwing up.

"Give me a minute. I'll think of something else."

"Uh, Tim?" I said gently. "I think Mrs. Kilton wants you to look up islands similar to ours, and write down the kinds of foods found there. I don't think she wants you to guess."

Tim's face fell. "Really? Aw, this is going to be a real drag."

Kallana snorted. "No kidding." She pushed her hair back from her face, causing the many silver bangles on her wrist to jingle, and slid a *Teen* magazine from her leather backpack.

"Ooh, let me see," Amy said. "There's supposed to be an article on Tara Lipinski in that issue."

"Really?" I said, then caught myself. "Wait a minute. We're supposed to be working." Tim and

Jaspal got up and wandered over to the encyclopedias.

"Later," Kallana said. "There's plenty of time before the bell." She stood up. "I'm going to look at the magazines. Maybe they've got the new *Teen Beat*."

I frowned and glanced at Amy.

"What?" Amy said. "Go ahead and work." She turned deliberately away and began flipping through the magazine.

I looked at her steadily. Amy was inviting me to confront her. I realized in a millisecond this was not just about a social studies project.

"Forget it, Amy," I said.

"Forget what?" She didn't bother to look up.

"The project. Forget trying to get out of doing the work. I'm not going to do the whole thing myself."

This time she lifted her head. "So don't." Her voice had a hard edge.

"So either the whole group fails, or Mrs. Kilton finds out that you slacked." I felt the anger rise in my chest.

"You going to tell her?" Amy asked.

I hesitated.

"Everybody hates a snitch, Jennie," Amy pressed. "Besides, I'm not the only one not doing any work. Look at Kallana and Tim."

"That's not the point! If the group fails, we could flunk this whole reporting period. My parents would kill me, and I won't be allowed to skate."

orted. "That would be a tragedy, all right."

clenched involuntarily. "Listen, Amy," I

missed. This isn't about a social studies project. This about your problem with me on the ice, and I'm pretty sick of it. So why don't you just spit it out?"

Amy gave me a level stare. "We don't have a problem on the ice. Unless it's yours."

I felt my face turn hot. "That's a total lie! You never miss the chance to show me up, tell me how badly I'm skating. We used to be best friends, Amy. Friends forever, we said. Remember that?" I couldn't keep the malice from my voice.

"That was a long time ago," Amy said through clenched teeth. "Things have changed."

"I'll say they have! You decided that I wasn't cool enough to hang out with in junior high. I'm not as pretty as you, I don't have the right clothes, so automatically I'm a geek. So much for loyalty!"

I was surprised to see Amy's chin wobble. She snatched up her books angrily.

"You don't know what you're talking about, Jennie. You don't have any idea," she said. "You think I care about those things? You think I care how you or anybody else looks? Which T-shirt goes with which jeans?" She shook her head. "You don't know me at all. You don't understand anything." Her voice got louder. Everyone in the library jerked their heads up. Their stares made my cheeks burn, but Amy seemed oblivious. "You're the one who is the perfect skating princess. Everything is just wonderful for *you*!"

"What?" I said. But Amy whirled around, stomped toward the doors and disappeared into the hallway.

Mrs. Kilton came over and touched my shoulder. "What's going on, Jennie?"

I shook my head. "I wish I knew."

"Come with me." She hurried out of the library door. "Amy, stop right there." Mrs. Kilton's whisper was a furious hiss. "Do you want to explain to me what that little display was all about in there?"

Amy shot me a venomous look. "I'd rather not say."

"Well, you'd better say something. Disrupting the class like that and running off into the hall is not something I appreciate. Now, if there's a problem, girls, I want to discuss it," Mrs. Kilton said, regaining a measure of calm.

Amy and I eyed each other silently.

"Girls?" Mrs. Kilton pressed. "Please tell me what's going on. Both of you are good students, and I'd never have expected this kind of behavior from you. Obviously something is wrong."

Amy's eyes hardened, and I felt my jaw clench. I wasn't going to try and explain how my former best friend had turned on me. If Mrs. Kilton wanted answers, Amy could provide them. But Amy obviously had no intention of speaking, either.

Mrs. Kilton sighed, just as the bell began to ring.

"All right," she said over the clanging. "I can't force you to talk about it. Just make sure you act appropriately in my class from now on. Any more shouting or running out of the room, and you both will take a trip to the principal's office. Understand?"

We nodded stiffly. Then as students poured into the halls, Amy wormed her way into the crowd, and I was left beside the library door, wondering just what exactly this fight was all about.

⑨ Rival at the Rink

Okay, Jennie. Let's run through your short program, then we'll work on your double Axel before we try the long program," Kate said, warming her hands on a mug of hot chocolate.

"Sure." I eyed the hot chocolate enviously as I skated to centre ice. It was 5:30 a.m. and my body felt sluggish and cold in the chilly rink, especially after such a lousy night's sleep. I'd kept thinking about Amy and the big scene in the library yesterday afternoon, until long after midnight. There had been something about the way she'd acted that made me feel guilty, and I didn't quite know why.

I shook my head and tried to concentrate on skating. Gliding to centre ice, I took my opening position and waited for the music. I was fairly confident with my short program. I'd been working on it for nearly four months, and it was about as close to perfect as I could get it.

As I skated through the required elements, I concentrated hard on making the spins tight and centred, and the jumps clean. My footwork was polished and precise; I could feel my body flow easily through the movements.

"Nicely done, Jennie!" Kate cried as I spun to a finish. "That kind of performance should put you in the medals for sure at Sectionals."

"Thanks." I couldn't keep the grin off my face. It felt so great to skate well.

"Okay. Just a couple of things …" Kate began.

I rolled my eyes. I'd just delivered a great short program, and Kate still had corrections.

She noticed my expression. "Unless the judges give you perfect scores, there's always something to improve, Jennie. As I was saying, you need to extend your back leg more on the landing of all your jumps. Keep your knee straight. And watch your arms as you land. You tend to stiffen, and that makes the jump look less graceful, less effortless. Okay?"

"Yes." I answered, barely stopping myself from adding "ma'am" with a salute. I didn't think Kate would appreciate the joke.

"Good. Other than those minor points, I thought you looked terrific. Let's give that double Axel a try."

I felt ready for anything. Confident, I chose a place in the rink that was open and began to circle toward it. I passed Amy, who stopped working on her double loop to watch. Immediately I froze up. I told myself I was being ridiculous, that Amy had watched me practise jumps for the last five years, but it was no use. Tension flowed through me like an electric wire, and as I powered into the jump, I couldn't get the height I needed. One revolution and I was down on the ice with both feet. At least I didn't fall, I consoled myself.

"Jennie, what was that? My grandmother could jump higher with a pair of lead boots on!" Kate frowned.

"I know, I know," I muttered.

"Try it again." Kate said.

Once more the tension made me freeze up, and no matter how much I forced myself to concentrate, I couldn't make the jump.

"Again!" shouted Kate.

I did the jump over and over again, but my technique was still off and I never landed it once.

Kate raked her hands through her short brown hair in exasperation. "I thought we were close to having this thing nailed," she said. "But it looks like we have a lot more work to do."

I swallowed. "I can do it, Kate. Today's just not my day."

"I hope so," she replied. "Because Sectionals is only a week away We don't have time to fiddle around with new parts of your long program. It has to be solid."

"It will be," I promised.

Kate frowned skeptically. "I hope so." She glanced at her watch. "I wanted to have time to run through the long program this morning, but we're out of lesson time. We'll have to do it this afternoon. Keep working on the Axel."

"Okay." I found a patch of ice to myself and began to circle. My backward crossovers were crisp and powerful, and when I lifted into the air, I whirled into the two rotations. I'd finally gotten the height I needed, but somehow my position was wrong, because my skates flew out from under me and I thudded painfully to the ice.

I sat there for a moment, stunned. Then I slowly got to my feet, and rubbing my sore backside, headed for the bleachers. A few minutes off the ice and a hot chocolate might help, I thought. I slipped my skate guards over the blades and clumped carefully toward the exit where the snack bar was located. I took care to keep out of Kate's view, because I knew she'd have a conniption if she saw me wasting practice time. Especially just before Sectionals.

"Hi, Mr. Ling," I said to the man behind the counter, as I pushed my change toward him. "Just a plain hot chocolate, please."

"No whipped cream today, Jennie?" Mr. Ling asked.

"No thanks. I don't have enough money. But that's okay." I said.

Mr. Ling added a dollop of whipped cream, anyway. "No charge," he said. "I know it's your favourite."

"Thank you." I smiled at him and took the cup, nearly dropping it when I turned and saw Amy standing right behind me.

Amy didn't move. I hesitated, holding the styrofoam cup carefully. There didn't seem to be much to say. We looked at each other steadily, then I heard myself asking the question that had bothered me for so long.

"What have I done to make you hate me so much?" I blurted. The words flew out of my mouth before I could stop them. But deep inside, a small part of me was relieved to finally say it out loud.

Amy turned away. "I don't hate you."

"Then why do keep you acting like such a jerk?" I said.

Amy's jaw tightened and she looked angry. "You would never understand. And I'm not a jerk."

"Well, you give a pretty good imitation of one," I said sarcastically. "You do everything you can to make my life a nightmare. You tease me at school, you bug me about how I skate, and you hang out with Kallana, who wouldn't know how to be nice to someone if they gave her written directions. Why?"

She stared straight at me. "I'm not telling you anything."

"Why? Amy, come on. Don't you remember making skating skirts out of my mom's old evening dresses and pretending we were famous? Don't you remember when we signed up for skating lessons and wanted to try jumping on the first day? Don't you remember last year, talking about that crush you had on Sam Hanlen? Sending notes in class? That secret code we invented in fifth grade? Come on, Amy." My chin quivered. "We've been friends for almost six years. Doesn't that count for something?"

Amy gulped. "I … I can't say it. You'll hate me."

"No, I won't."

"I …" Amy fiddled with the zipper on her sweatshirt. "I can't stand being around you."

"What?" I said, stung. "Why?"

"Not the way you think. It's because of skating. Geez, Jennie, you have everything. How do you think I feel? You have a nice boyfriend, you're smart, you have a great family. Do you know that my dad has never once come to a skating competition? Not once. Your dad is at every one. But I'm still supposed to win, or it's not good enough." Amy gulped again. "And the most important thing of all — you are a great skater. Not just good, like me. Great. I've heard all the rumours — what Kate says about you, how you're destined for the Olympics and everything."

She clenched her hands into fists. "The rotten thing is, it's true! I can see that it's true. So I just keep skating my butt off hoping that it will pay off someday, but I know in the end it won't because I don't have one-tenth of the talent that you have. Even though I work about four times as hard as you do, I'll never be as good as you." Amy paused and made a strangled sound as she took a breath. "It's not fair!"

I blinked. "You believe all that?"

"I just said so, didn't I?" Amy said. She leaned against the cinder block wall, trying hard to keep her face neutral.

"Amy, you … you're wrong." I struggled to find the right words. "Things aren't perfect for me at all."

She raised her eyebrows.

"I mean it," I said. "Kyle isn't my boyfriend. He's practically the only friend I have, since you dumped me. All I ever do is skate. I don't have time to make friends at school, and since you and Kallana decided I'm completely uncool, hardly anyone wants to be friends with me anyway."

"Oh," Amy said.

"And I feel like a total geek most of the time at school. I thought that's why you didn't want to be friends anymore, because now you're so popular and everything. And Kallana makes me feel like a reject from a rummage sale, with her designer wardrobe."

Amy's lips curved into an unwilling half-smile. "You're not the only one."

"And my family … yeah, they're supportive. So supportive that they don't understand that I'm not sure that a career in skating is for me. I'm not even sure if my dad would even let me quit if I wanted to."

"You're thinking of quitting skating?" Amy looked shocked.

"I don't know. Not really, I guess, because I love skating. But I'm not absolutely sure that I want to be so competitive, and that's the point. And yeah, it feels great to finally have Kate tell me that I have what it takes to *maybe* be one of the best, after dreaming about it since I was a little kid." I said slowly. "But the thing is, the reality is not exactly what we pictured when we were eight years old. For starters, I'll have to practise so much that I won't have a life beyond the rink. Kyle asked me to go see Elvis Stojko two weeks ago, and Kate wouldn't let me miss practice. That's just the way it is if you want to be the best. And the competition is so tough, I don't know if I want that kind of pressure. I'm not sure if it's worth it."

Amy was silent for a moment. "I don't know. I think it would be worth it. To be the best, I mean."

I chewed on my bottom lip. "Remember how we used to practise together after lessons last year? What happened to that?"

"Well —" Amy frowned. "I stopped wanting to, I guess. I just can't help trying to be better than you on the ice. Especially since last summer, when you really started getting good."

"That's exactly what I mean," I sighed. "We started

to compete, and suddenly we couldn't be friends. Why? Why does it have to be like that?"

"I don't know. It just does, I guess," Amy said. "It's hard not to think of you as someone I have to beat in meets."

I was silent for a moment. "I wish it could be different."

Amy hesitated. "I don't think it ever will."

10 Looking for Answers

Where were you during practice this morning, Jennie?" Dad turned the car's ignition, and the headlights splashed their beams against the ice rink's grey stone wall. "I meant to ask where you disappeared to." Dad shifted gears and we headed toward home.

I stared out the window into the dusk and shifted my skate bag between my ankles. "Um, I went to get a hot chocolate from Mr. Ling."

"For half an hour?" Dad shook his head. "Jennie, you can't afford to lose that kind of practice time goofing off, and I can't afford to pay for it. You know how much ice time costs."

"I worked hard at practice this afternoon."

"That's not the point. You didn't work hard this morning. And I noticed you're having a lot of trouble with that jump again. What is it — the double Lutz? I thought you were supposed to use that at Sectionals."

"It's the double Axel. And I *am* using it in Sectionals." My voice was hardly above a whisper. I didn't think I could stand much more criticism. I was still thinking about my talk with Amy, and the pressure to land that jump had made the afternoon practice a shambles.

We pulled up to the house. Dad hit the button on the garage door opener and eased the car inside, manoeuvering to avoid Dylan's toboggan, BMX bike, and skateboard. "You'll never land it if you keep on the way you are."

"Dad, I'm trying," I protested, getting out and slamming the car door.

"I know, honey. I'm just saying that I don't think you should be wasting your ice time when you have so much work to do to get ready for Sectionals."

"It was just one lousy hot chocolate! Can't you give me a break?" My voice rose.

"Sure I can, but I don't think the judges will." Dad calmly held the screen door open so I could wedge past him with my over-stuffed skate bag.

"Don't think the judges will what?" Mom asked. She was peeling Dylan's muddy ski jacket off. "Look at this mess. Next time the Johnson twins want you to go tobogganing, make sure the whole hill has snow on it, okay, Dylan? You look like you've been swimming in a mud pit."

"The hill had snow when we started," Dylan

argued. "But there were so many kids sliding, it all got pushed to the bottom."

I would have laughed if I hadn't been in such a bad mood. Dylan looked so funny — he had twigs stuck in his hair, and his face was smudged with dirt. "If there isn't any snow, how could you keep sliding?" I wanted to know, thankful he had provided an interruption.

"Frozen mud works pretty good," he answered cheerfully. "But it's kind of easy to wipe out, 'cause you can't steer."

Mom groaned. "Go wash up, Dylan." As he trotted down the hall, she turned back to me. "So anyway, what was that about the judges?"

My stomach tightened up again.

"Jennie and I were just talking about Sectionals. She took a rather long break from practice this morning, and we were discussing the value of ice time," Dad answered.

I glared at him. He didn't have to give Mom the details, and now I was in for another lecture.

"Oh, Jennie, you didn't! You know better than that," Mom scolded.

"I just wanted a hot chocolate," I protested.

Dad's mouth twitched, like he was swallowing a smile. "Must have been a big one, because it took her half an hour to drink it."

"Half an hour!" Mom looked at me. "Jennie what were you thinking?"

I rubbed my forehead. "Not about skating, exactly."

"I guess not. Jennie, you know how important it is to use the ice time."

I rounded on her. "Yes, I do! And I'm sick of hearing about it," I snapped, my patience at an end.

"Jennie —" Mom started, but I cut her off.

"Dad spent the whole ride home yelling at me about practice this morning, and I don't feel like hearing it all over again, okay?" I shouted.

"Jennie, I didn't yell," Dad said. "Now just calm down. I wanted to make sure you got the point."

"I got the point, all right. But what about you? Do you really know what's going on? How I feel? Do you even care? All everybody keeps talking about around here is how Kate thinks I'm going to be the next Canadian Olympic medalist, and nobody ever asks me how I feel about it!"

Mom was silent, and Dad looked taken aback. "Well, how *do* you feel?"

I took a deep breath. "I don't know. Scared, I guess. I'm not sure if I really want to do it."

"That's natural, Jennie," Dad said. "Of course you'd feel a little unsure. That level of competition is really tough."

"You don't understand," I said wearily. "It's not skating so much … it's other things."

"Like what?" Dad said.

I looked around and realized how ridiculous this was. We were all standing in the front hallway, my father and I were still in our winter boots and ski jackets, and my mother was still holding Dylan's filthy, mud-globbed coat. Nobody had even moved since I'd come in the door. Everyone's attention was focused on me, as usual. I suddenly found it stifling. "Can we eat?" I asked quietly. "I'm really hungry."

Mom looked surprised. "Of course. Come on. I've got baked ravioli in the oven."

Dad hung up his jacket. "I don't think we're finished talking about this yet."

"Later, John." Mom studied my face. "Give her a few minutes."

It wasn't until I'd finished my last bite of ravioli and drained the milk from my glass that Mom would let my dad bring up the subject again. Dylan was playing a video game in the family room, which left the kitchen conveniently clear.

"Okay, Jennie, I want to know how my giving you heck for slacking off at practice has led to you talking about quitting skating," Dad said.

"I'm not talking about quitting, exactly. I'm just not sure that I want to go to the Olympics and all that."

"Okay. Why not? It's what you've talked about since you were six years old."

I felt defeated. "I know. But it's not how I expected it to be …"

"You thought maybe you could just climb up on the podium without working for it?" Dad asked.

"No! I just — Dad, you don't understand!" I said angrily. "I'm not lazy, you know. I wouldn't have gotten up at five a.m. for the last two years to go to the rink if I were."

"I know," Dad said. "But you're right, I don't understand. What *is* going on?"

"Well," I began. The whole thing seemed difficult to put into words. "The first thing is, school has been awful. There's this girl, Kallana Ohlmstead, who is really a pain in the neck, and she makes me feel like a complete idiot. What's worse though, is a lot of girls want to be friends with her, because she always dresses really cool, and always has the right thing to say to the boys and stuff."

"So?" Dad looked puzzled, but Mom placed her hand on his knee.

"Wait," she said. "I think I understand."

"So, anyway, I feel really out of it at school, and I never have time to do things with the other kids after class, because I always have skating practice."

"Can't you make friends at skating?" Dad wanted to know.

"Sure. But everybody is always so busy practising their own routines, we never really have time for fun together. And the one person who could have been my friend — *was* my friend — is so competitive that she can't even see me as a person. I'm just her enemy on the ice."

"Amy?" Mom asked.

"Yes." There was no point hiding it any longer. "And now Amy hangs out with Kallana."

"Why didn't you tell us? I wondered why you and Amy weren't spending time together any more, but you never seemed to want to talk about it."

"Well, I'm telling you now. Amy has acted like she hated me ever since skating camp last summer, and it's all because she wants to be a great skater — the best skater — more than she wants anything else, including my friendship."

"Oh Jen," Mom said softly. Her voice was so laden with sympathy, I nearly started to cry.

"Honey, you're going to have to handle tough relationships with other skaters sometimes. That can happen when you start to compete at elite levels," Dad said.

"Yeah, but I don't like dealing with this stuff, and it's only going to get harder if I keep skating. I'm not sure I want that."

"Do you still like skating?" Mom asked.

"Yes. I love being on the ice, and I like challenging myself, to see if I can make the jumps and do the spins. And Kate is a really good coach."

"If you still want to skate, instead of dealing with Amy or whoever else is causing problems, then you should. Skating is skating, not all that other garbage," Dad said.

"But skating *is* about the other things," Mom protested. "You can't just ignore the politics or the competition or the rivalries, John. That's like saying your work has nothing to do with the people you deal with day after day," Mom said. "It would be nice if sports were just purely the sport itself, but there's so much more to it. And the successful athletes are the ones who learn to deal with it and still excel."

"True," Dad admitted, "but I still think if Jennie concentrates on her skating and blocks out everything else —"

"Dad, I've just been telling you that I have no social life at school because of skating, and now you're telling me I should have no social life at skating. Not that I do," I added, "but I'm trying to say that friends are important to me, and I have no time. And it seems like I can't make friends at skating, because we're either too busy competing with each other, or just too busy, period."

"Okay. But would someone please explain to me what this all has to do with skipping half of practice this morning?"

"When I went to get my hot chocolate, I saw Amy. We ended up talking about the argument we had at school yesterday."

"And …?" Mom asked.

"And she said pretty much what I just told you. She doesn't want to be friends anymore. I'm her rink rival, and that's it."

Mom and Dad heaved a collective sigh. "There's no easy answers to this, Jenzo," Dad said. "It's a tough decision. Would you really want to give up competitive skating for a normal teenage life?"

I frowned. "I don't know."

"I hate that phrase," Mom said suddenly. "A normal teenage life — what is normal, anyway? And what makes everyone so sure that 'normal' is so much better or happier than extraordinary?"

I shook my head in confusion. "I don't get it, Mom."

She put her arm around me. "Never mind. It's just another way of saying the grass is always greener on the other side of the fence."

"I feel like all I do is skate, sleep and go to school. I know I love skating, but I want to feel like I'm a part of things too. I want friends."

"Can you have both?" Mom asked.

"I don't know," I said slowly. "I just don't know."

11 Kallana and the Homework Patrol

"Hi, Jennie," Jaspal gave me a quiet grin. "Here's my part of the project."

"Thanks, Jas," I tucked it in with my portion and Tim's. "That's three of us who finished, anyway."

"Make that four," Amy slid a stapled sheaf of notepaper onto my desk. It was covered with Amy's meticulous handwriting. I looked up in surprise. She shrugged. "I had time after practice."

I smiled. "Thanks, Amy." She almost smiled back, but then Kallana dropped into the seat across the aisle.

"So, how's the report coming?" Kallana asked. She tucked her straw-blond hair behind her ears and tilted her head as though she were posing for a magazine cover. Today she wore faded olive-green jeans and a loose, soft tweed blazer over an oatmeal-coloured waffle-knit T-shirt. The sleeves of the blazer were rolled up to her elbows, and she looked like she was ready for a horseback ride in the English countryside. She looked so perfect, so "in," so cool, I could only stare for a moment. Then I was acutely conscious of my no-name blue sweatshirt and baggy jeans. I felt a stab of jealousy, and that made me angry. I was tired of this superficial war.

"Actually, Kallana, it's finished," I said sweetly.

"Great!" Kallana leaned back in her seat to reveal polished brown ankle boots. "For a while I thought we weren't going to get it all together."

"It's finished," I said, "except for your part."

Kallana sat up. "My part? What do you mean? We all worked on this together, right?"

"No. We divided up the questions so we each had some to do. You were reading magazines in the library, so I guess maybe you didn't hear," I said.

"Well, why didn't someone tell me?" she demanded.

"If you had worked on the project with us, you would have known," I said quietly.

Kallana stared at me. "What is this, the homework patrol?" she jeered. "Give me a break. How do I know what you guys are doing?"

"Well, why shouldn't you know?" I asked. "It's your project, too. You're part of the group, right?"

Kallana looked at Amy.

"I did remind you about the homework. After school, remember?" Amy said. I glanced at her, surprised by this unexpected support. I'd figured Amy would stick with Kallana, and I'd wind up feeling like a complete idiot.

"I forgot. So sue me." Kallana shrugged, her voice heavy with sarcasm. "This is still a group project."

Tim looked anxious, and Jas glanced at me. I took a deep breath.

"This is still a group project, but you're not part of it, Kallana. You didn't do any of the work."

"So who's going to know?" Kallana challenged. "Unless you tell." The unspoken meaning of Kallana's words was obvious. Nobody hangs out with a snitch, Jennie. Where had I heard those words before?

I kept my voice steady. "I don't have to tell anybody anything. Mrs. Kilton knows we divided the work in the project among the five of us, and everybody's handwriting is on the section they did. All except yours. You think Mrs. Kilton is so dumb she won't notice?"

For once, Kallana had no reply.

"Maybe you'd better go ask Mrs. Kilton for an extension on this report," I said.

Kallana stood up with one quick motion. "You win this time, Jennie," she hissed. "But I won't forget. You can count on it."

★ ★ ★

The cafeteria was jammed, and the greasy smell of french fries and hot dogs rose from behind the hot lunch counter. I wrinkled my nose and headed toward the sandwiches. I didn't feel much like eating. The scene with Kallana had left my stomach tied up in knots. Would she try to get back at me? What could she do? Spread rumours? Try and make everyone hate me?

I caught sight of Amy halfway across the cafeteria. To my surprise, she waved and began to weave through chairs and kids to reach me in line.

"Hi, Jennie!" she said. "I was watching for you." She slipped behind me in line.

"Hey, no butting," the two boys behind me growled.

Amy turned and gave them her prettiest smile. "Sorry. But this is really important. I just need to talk to her."

"Yeah, right," they said, but they didn't protest.

"What are you doing?" I asked her in a low voice. "If Kallana sees you talking to me, she'll be majorly ticked off. You're in enemy territory now, you know."

Amy grimaced, grabbing a roast beef sandwich from the stack in front of us. "It doesn't matter. She's mad at me too, because I did the homework for the report and handed it in with you guys." Amy shrugged. "What was I supposed to do, fail? Just because Kallana didn't feel like doing her homework? Forget it."

"Don't you care if she's mad?" I wondered.

"She'll get over it. She's always mad at somebody. She was just steaming after class," Amy said.

Terrific. Exactly what I wanted to hear.

Amy saw the expression on my face. "Don't worry. Kallana's not the boss of everybody in the world, even if she thinks she is. She likes to be in control. That's why it's so funny when someone stands up to her. She gets totally warped. But what can she do? Nothing."

"I can think of a few things," I said.

Amy shook her head. "No, she won't do anything dumb. It would look bad if kids found out she tried to bully the whole group into doing her work for her. Besides, you stood up to her once, she'll be afraid you'll do it again. Now she knows she can't push you around."

"I guess." I wasn't convinced.

"Hey! Let's move!" someone shouted. "Some of us want to eat!"

I yanked a tray from the stack and slid it along the cafeteria counter. "Do you really like hanging out with Kallana?"

Amy hesitated, her expression suddenly guarded. "Um … yeah, I do. She can be a real snob, but she can also be really fun. She knows everything about fashion, so shopping with her is a blast."

"Hmmm."

"The thing is, since her parents split up, she hardly

ever sees her dad, and her mom is totally wrapped up in her business," Amy tried to explain. "They just buy her tons of stuff to make up for it. And sometimes I think Kallana tries to be like some teen supermodel, to get her mom to pay attention to her. There are pictures of beautiful models stacked all over their house, and I bet Kallana feels gross, compared to them. I know I would." Amy covered her mouth with one hand. "She'd kill me if she knew I told you this stuff."

"I won't say anything," I said. "But I still think she's a bully. Does she think she's better than other people by making them feel like geeks?"

"I don't know," Amy said uncomfortably. "All I know is, when we hang out, she can be really fun. Besides, geeky people should smarten up and learn how to be cool."

"Maybe Kallana isn't cool at all, underneath all those fancy clothes and that fake confidence. Maybe inside she's just as big a geek as Tim Dupries, and she's scared stiff someone will find out," I said viciously. "Maybe that's why she's so nasty all the time, because if she lets too many people find out what you just told me, they'll realize that she's just as uncool as the rest of us. She just hides it well."

I grabbed a veggie sandwich and a carton of chocolate milk, and pushed my tray toward the cash register. After paying the cashier, Amy and I stopped and looked at each other, holding our loaded lunch trays. I thought about asking her if she wanted to eat lunch together. I wondered if she was thinking the same thing, but I suddenly felt awkward, and Amy stared down at her tray.

"Well … uh … see you at the rink this afternoon," I said. I just couldn't ask her if she'd sit with me. I was too scared she'd say no.

"Yeah." I thought I saw a flicker of loneliness in Amy's eyes, but it was gone almost instantly, and her smile was forced, unyielding. "I'll be there."

12 Kate Takes Over

Come on, Jennie. Get on the ice!" Kate yelled.

I slowly removed my skate guards and took an extra minute to stretch my hamstrings, lower back and shoulders.

"Jennie, let's go!" Kate bellowed.

Amy tugged at the skirt of her rose-coloured skating dress. An uneasy silence hung between us. I stepped stiffly out onto the ice.

Kate leaned against the boards at the far end of the rink. "Okay, let's go through the first part of your long program, right up to the double Axel."

I nodded and skated to centre ice. I linked my hands and folded my arms so my chin rested on my fingers, elbows slanted in a diagonal line, my body twisted and curved into a dramatic pose.

Kate looked at me critically. "Jennie, loosen up. You look like a pretzel."

I tried to make the position look more relaxed,

graceful. Instead, I felt tighter than ever inside. The music began, and I began to skate. But instead of the flowing movements and the concise, clean footwork required in the routine, my body performed a series of jerky steps like a marionette with tangled strings. I turned and began the back crossovers to lead into my double Axel. I hesitated, and before I began the jump, the music was cut off.

I looked up in surprise.

Kate stepped away from the music system and beckoned me over to the boards. "I thought I'd save you the agony," she said. "I knew you were going to reduce it to a single."

"I didn't have the momentum," I said.

"No, what you didn't have was the concentration," Kate answered sternly. "And you haven't had it all week. Now tell me the truth, Jennie. What's going on?"

I glanced involuntarily at Amy, who was pulling out of a sitspin, then I stared at the ice. "I don't know. Stress, I guess."

Kate regarded me tensely, then turned and skated off the ice. "Come with me," she called back over her shoulder. "You too, Amy." Amy looked startled at being summoned during my lesson, but followed us obediently off the ice. Kate slipped on skate guards and clumped through the rink doors to her small office in the arena lobby. "Okay. I'm not sure what's going on with you guys, but neither of you has performed well this week, and with Sectionals coming up, I want to get to the bottom of it. So spill it. Fighting? Raging jealousy? Personality conflict? Practical jokes involving paint in the shower or stink bombs in your locker? Come on, you can tell me. I can stand it."

Amy and I looked at each other. "No. We're not fighting," we said.

"At least, not anymore," I added.

"Okay. Why not?" Kate asked.

"Why not what?" I said.

"Why aren't you fighting anymore, and why were you fighting in the first place? And why, if you're not fighting, are the two of you, my best novice skaters, performing like goony birds on popsicle sticks?"

I smothered a smile. "Well, we were fighting because …" I trailed off.

"Because …" Amy swallowed hard. "I've been majorly jealous. Of Jennie, that is. And I didn't want to be friends anymore."

"And you do now?" Kate asked.

Amy hesitated. "Well … I don't know," she admitted.

I felt a stab of hurt. "Why?" I said.

"I don't know if I can stop competing with you! You have my dream, and I want it!" she burst out. There was a silence, then Amy rubbed her eyes with the back of her sleeve. The quiet in the office was broken by the faint yells of the hockey team in the rink across the lobby. "Why," Amy said, "does everyone pay so much attention to you? It's like you're the star and I'm just in the background somewhere."

I felt terribly guilty. "I can't help it. I'd be lying if I said I wasn't glad Kate told me I have all this talent, and she thinks I'll make it to the top."

Amy sniffled.

"I just don't see why we have to feel like enemies as soon as we're on the ice. We'd get a lot further if we just helped each other at practice," I pointed out.

"I know that," Amy said, her voice suddenly snappish. "And I've tried that, but you got all snotty on me, so I gave up."

I remember the time Amy had corrected me on my flying camel. "That's because you were competing with me. You were trying to show how much better you could do the spin than I could."

"I was not!"

"Girls, please," Kate held up her hand.

A heavy silence fell. Kate finally spoke. "This is part of sports, you guys. Part of figure skating. If you concentrate on hating the people who are better skaters than you, you'll create a lot of enemies. And you'll miss out on valuable training opportunities. You can learn from skaters who are better, and become a stronger skater yourself. Everyone who is serious about the sport knows what it's like to feel jealous," Kate said. "But you have to learn to deal with it, and concentrate on your own work, your own successes. Not everyone is going to win Olympic gold. Not everyone will make it to Nationals. Not everyone will win parts in Ice Capades."

"But what if you want to be a great skater so badly, you feel like you'll die if you don't get it?" Amy said.

Kate smiled. "Then you work hard, keep trying, keep learning. The best skaters in the world are the ones who never gave up."

Amy considered. "Yes, I guess that's true."

Kate laid a hand on my shoulder and reached for Amy's. "The point is, what are you two going to do about your competition on the ice?"

I swallowed and looked at Amy. "I'd like to be friends again, Ames."

She sighed. "Yeah, me too. Maybe we can try to forget about competitions and stuff while we're practising. I can try, I guess, but I don't know."

"I do," Kate said. "The better you get at skating, Amy, the less you'll feel like you have to compete with Jennie. And Jennie, Ms. Super-Skater, if you don't keep working as hard as Amy, you're going to find your butt at the bottom of the placings. Got that?"

Amy and I laughed. "Yes, ma'am," I said, giving Kate a mock salute.

"Good. Then get those sorry behinds of yours back on the ice. We're wasting practice time!"

13 Amy Skates

My heart sank as I ran my finger down the list of names. The Sectionals short program results had just been posted, and I was third. I knew my combination jump had been shaky, I had missed a few cues in the music for the spins, and my timing had been off. But I didn't think it had affected my performance to that extent. Amy had finished with a strong score that put her in second place, just barely ahead of me. I smiled grimly, knowing I would have to pull out all the stops if I wanted to place first overall. The short program counted for one third of the total score, so it was still possible for me to win, but I would have to be perfect.

I gathered my skate bag up and pushed through the knot of skaters clustered around the posting. Inside the locker room, I stripped off my leggings and sweatshirt and carefully pulled on a pair of nylons. Then I slid my skating dress over my head and zipped up the back before surveying myself in the mirror. The dress was beautiful — a deep garnet-red stretch velvet, trimmed with gold braid around the sweetheart neck-line and the cuffs of the long sleeves. The short skirt fell in graceful folds over my hips, and the bodice clung tightly to my waist. I touched the soft material and smiled.

"You look beautiful, Jennie," Mom suddenly appeared beside me.

"Thanks for making the dress, Mom." The velvet felt smooth and warm against my skin.

"You and Dad did a lot of the work, too," Mom said, hugging me.

"I know." I couldn't stop staring at myself. Mom had made lots of skating costumes for me, but this was my first truly grown-up looking dress. Dad and I had helped cut out the material and sew on the gold braid, but Mom had fitted the bodice and sewn the tucks expertly into the skirt. The deep red color glowed against my skin, and made my dark curly hair look even darker. I smoothed a curl back into the knot of hair at the nape of my neck. Everything looked perfect.

Now if I could only skate the same way.

Kate poked her head into the locker room. "Jennie, it's almost time to warm up."

"Okay," I called, feeling a nervous fluttering in my stomach. After the discussion with Amy and Kate, I felt better about skating than I had in days, but I still wasn't sure I'd be able to land the double Axel. In practice,

I'd nailed it about fifty per cent of the time — not enough to count on getting it perfect during a competition.

I pulled on my skate guards and clumped toward the locker room door. Amy met me, and for a second avoided my eyes. Then she looked up. "Good luck, Jennie," she said.

"Same to you, Ames." I smiled. "You look great." Amy wore a silvery-blue skating dress with a wispy chiffon skirt.

"So do you." She eyed me competitively. "See you out there."

I moved toward the rink and shook my head as I stretched. Amy would always compete. And truthfully, so would I. Inside, I was resisting the temptation to meet her challenge. If we both wanted to skate *and* be friends, we were going to have to keep reminding ourselves that being rivals was not the same thing as being enemies. Kate had told us that sometimes a healthy rivalry helps skaters excel, but that hating each other doesn't help anyone.

"Flight A novice warm-up will begin in five minutes," a voice blared over the loudspeaker. "Five minutes for flight A novice warm-up, please."

Kate zipped a jacket over her turtleneck sweater. "It's chilly in here today," she said, clapping her hands together. "Be sure you wrap up after the warm-up. Keep your muscles loose. That goes for you too, Amy," she added as Amy appeared from the locker room behind me.

I rolled my shoulders and gently stretched my neck, then stepped out onto the ice.

"Jennie, try the flying camel and a sitspin, first, then go through all the jumps," Kate directed. "Amy, start with a spiral, then I want to see a toe loop."

I turned away from Amy and found a clean patch of ice where I could concentrate. I began stroking around the rink, then sailed into the flying camel. I nailed it right on, then pulled up into a scratch spin. Then I tried a sitspin; it felt tight and sure. I checked the clock to see how much warm-up time was left before I launched into a double flip-double flip combination. It felt steady, but not as high as I would like, but there was no time to repeat it. Hurriedly, I flew into a double loop. The height was better on this one, but I wobbled the landing. I pulled out of it and stopped.

"Jennie, pull your arms in tighter on the rotation," Kate called from the boards. "And watch the position of your back leg."

I nodded and decided to try the loop again, before attempting the double Axel. I wanted to feel sure of myself before I tried that jump. This time, as I lifted into the double loop, I could feel my body fly through the rotations cleanly and my skate touched down with precision. I smiled. That was how it was supposed to be. But the smile left my face as the whistle blew, signalling the end of the warm-up. As an official waved the skaters off the ice, I moved toward the boards, fighting panic.

"Kate," I hissed. "I never had time to try the Axel! Now what am I going to do?"

Kate looked thoughtful. "If you single it, you have to nail every single jump, including the combinations, to win. There are some very good competitors here."

Including Amy, I thought.

"And if you fall on the double, it could take you down enough to place low, anyway," she continued.

"This isn't much help," I complained.

"See how you feel on the ice. If you're nailing everything else, and you don't feel confident enough on the double, single it. But if you think you can land the double, go for it. I know you can do a double Axel perfectly if you want to, but you have to know it, too, or else …"

"Or else, what?" I gulped.

"Or else you'll mess it up," Kate said with a wry grin.

"Thanks," I said bitterly. "That's a lot of help." I sat down on the bench and wrapped a polar fleece jacket around my knees. I knew I'd have a while to wait. I was skating fifth. Amy was third.

"I think I'll wait in the locker room," Amy said nervously. "Can you come and get me when it's almost time, Kate?"

"Sure." Kate's eyes were glued to the activity among the judges. I remained where I was. It was always a temptation to watch the other competitors, one that I often fought against. Sometimes knowing how good the other skaters were spurred me to skate beyond my expectations. Other times, it made me so nervous, I could barely concentrate on my own routine.

I fished a magazine and my Walkman out of my bag, and slid in a tape of dance tunes. Plugging the headphones into my ears, I flipped through the magazine until I found an article that looked interesting and settled back to read. Even though I kept my eyes trained on the page, I found it hard not to notice what was happening on the ice. Still, I fought the impulse until I saw Amy fidgeting by the boards. I reached for the volume control and turned down the music, letting the magazine fall onto my lap.

"Flight A, skater number three, Amy Sehlmeier," said the loudspeaker.

A pert smile flashed on Amy's face and she stepped out on the ice. Gliding over to the middle of the rink, she took her opening pose.

"You shouldn't watch this," Mom whispered in my ear.

I know, I thought. But I couldn't take my eyes off of her. The music swelled from the speakers, and Amy seemed to dance across the ice. She grinned at the audience as though she didn't have a care in the world. As I watched, she landed a perfect single Axel, double Lutz combination.

"Jennie, you're up after the next skater," Kate whispered. "Stretch a bit and get ready." I pried my gaze away from the rink and nodded. As I made my way over to the boards, I noticed Amy, her chin uplifted, stroking past the judges and without a pause, whirling into a flying camel.

I swallowed. I'd have to work harder than I thought to beat her. I'd have to be absolutely perfect, especially if I singled the double Axel.

Amy finished her routine with a flourish, threw the judges a dazzling smile and skated off the ice. She stepped off the rink near Kate and me, and instantly the smile was replaced by an anxious frown. "How did I do, Kate?" she whispered. She was breathing hard, and little droplets of sweat ran down her temples.

"Great job!" Kate said, hugging her. "I think that's the best I've ever seen you skate." I handed Amy her warm-up jacket.

"Nice skate, Amy," I said. Even to me, my voice sounded flat.

Amy raised her eyebrows. "Thanks," she said. Kate shushed us both, waiting for Amy's marks. As they came up, Amy gave a little squeak of excitement. Her marks were high, higher than at other competitions. Amy had outdone herself, had improved without my being aware of it. And now I had a competitor for the Sectionals title.

At that uncertain moment, my name was called. "Kate!" I whispered frantically. "What's going on? I'm not supposed to be next."

Kate looked a little perplexed. "The other skater must have scratched, and it wasn't marked on my sheet." Scratching is the term used for athletes who drop out of a competition at the last minute. Sometimes it's because of an injury or other emergencies, but all I knew was that I had lost those last few minutes to prepare myself.

Kate glanced at my face. "Don't panic. You've warmed up and stretched. You're ready. Just do your best."

I took a deep breath, straightened my skirt and stepped onto the ice.

14 Promise of a Dream

The expanse of white ice gleamed under the lights. I clutched at the edge of the boards for one anxious moment before pushing off to the centre of the rink. My lips were quivering with nervousness, and I pressed them tightly together before remembering to smile. Instantly I manufactured a sickly grin and pasted it on.

"Come on, Jennie!" I thought. "You can do this! Concentrate!" But I still felt flustered, and my hands shook as I took my opening pose.

I closed my eyes, waiting for the music, and when the first few notes flowed over the loudspeakers, my hands miraculously steadied and the fear that tightened my stomach faded to a pleasant tingle. This was what I had been trained to do.

I picked up my feet in the light, intricate dance steps that opened the routine, then glided easily into a spiral, forcing my back leg high in the air. Then came a short footwork sequence before I began stroking down the rink to build up power for the double Lutz. An easy jump for me, I was grateful when I landed it, and the tight smile on my face relaxed a little.

But the routine wasn't going as smoothly as I had hoped. I managed to perform each jump and spin technically well, but I felt stiff and mechanical. I stumbled a little on some of the footwork, and in the back of my mind I was waiting for the double Axel. With such an uninspired performance, the single would not be enough to put me in first place.

I knew I had to try the double, but a cold lump in my stomach made me hesitate. For a split second I felt like I'd swallowed an icicle, and then it was over. I was whirling in the air too quickly to even think. Arms extended, I reached my back leg out to the ice, preparing for a solid landing, when the unthinkable happened. My skate slipped awkwardly out from under me and I crashed to the ice. The breath shot out from me in a sharp hiccup, and I lay there, stunned, gaping like a fish.

Only two thoughts occurred to me: first, if I couldn't get any air into my lungs, I would die right there in the middle of the rink, and second, I was in the middle of my routine, and I had to get up and keep going.

Someone stopped the music. As Kate ran out on the ice, the silence was embarrassing.

"Jennie, are you okay?" she asked, her eyes wide

with fear. I nodded, the breath coming back to me in a horrible, groaning wheeze. I sat up.

"Can you get up?" she said. I nodded again and braced myself against her as she pulled me to my feet. Between the sudden nausea and the little black dots that danced in front of my eyelids, I hardly realized that she was shuffling me toward the boards.

"No!" I said, pulling away. "I have to finish the routine."

"Jennie, don't be stupid. You could have a concussion."

"No." I could see clearly now and the nausea was fading. "I didn't hit my head or anything. I'm okay. I want to skate. Please, they'll disqualify me!"

"Jennie!"

"Please!"

Kate looked at me uncertainly. "Well, if you're sure you're okay …"

"I'm fine," I insisted.

"I'll talk to the judges. Maybe they'll let you skate from the beginning." Kate crossed the rink, and I edged over to the boards and hung on tightly.

"Jennie, what are you doing?" Dad made his way through the skaters. Mom was right behind him.

"I want to finish the routine." I needed to prove to myself that I could do it, that I could skate under pressure, that I could still do my best.

"Jennie, don't be a hero. This isn't the Olympics,"

Mom scolded. "You shouldn't skate until we know you're okay."

"I feel fine."

Kate was waving to me from across the rink. I skated toward her, and she caught me by my shoulder. "They're going to let you start from the beginning. I told them that you wanted to try again." She looked at me. "Are you sure you're okay?"

"Yes, I'm fine," I said impatiently. I wanted to skate. All my nervousness had disappeared, which seemed strange, since I'd just experienced one of the most embarrassing moments of my skating career so far. But instead of feeling self-conscious, an electric determination filled me. I couldn't keep my hands from clenching into stubborn fists. I needed to skate.

Kate gave me a last, concerned look. "Okay, get out there, then," she said.

I was intensely aware of the silence in the rink as I pushed off on the ice. No one moved as I took my opening position. Then the music began.

I felt strong. The footwork that began my program was crisper than before. I began to focus on audience — the people watching, the judges, Kate, my parents. I tried to pick out individual faces in the crowd, and I shot a bright smile at a little girl in a blue jacket who was craning her neck to see over the boards.

Each segment of the routine was so imbedded in my brain that I didn't even need to think about it. My body took over, and I began to enjoy the old elation of flying on the ice. Double flip-double flip combination, split jump, double loop — everything felt precise and clean and tight. My skates felt light, as though they were made out of air. I nailed every jump, and after each one I felt a surge of confidence. I could do this. This was my dream.

I began the approach to the double Axel. As I lifted into it, I felt as if time slowed down. Airborne, I saw the rinkside revolve slowly around and around, then I felt my skate touch the ice. I wobbled, but I held the landing. My last move, the flying camel sitspin — otherwise known as the death drop — was intended to finish the program on a dramatic note. With a last burst of energy, I launched high into a flying camel take-off, then reached for the ice with my right leg, and bent quickly into a sitspin position, the ice churning beneath my blade. Whirling around and around, I gradually stood up and pulled into a blinding scratch spin. I reached out, dug my toe pick into the ice and struck my final pose.

15 The Gold Medal

A dazzled, excited smile bubbled up from somewhere inside me and spread across my face. I'd landed the double Axel! I'd actually landed it in a competition, when it really counted. I gave my mom and dad a huge grin and glided off the ice.

"Excellent skate, Jennie!" Kate beamed at me as I stepped out of the rink and grabbed me in a one-armed hug. The other arm pressed her clipboard anxiously to her chest as we waited for the marks.

As the marks came up, I searched Kate's face. They were close to Amy's, but were they better?

Kate answered the question in my eyes. "I can't tell, Jennie. Amy gave a pretty spectacular performance. We'll have to wait until they calculate the placings."

Amy stood on the other side of Kate, waiting quietly. She twisted the hem of her skating skirt around her fingers, tightening the fabric, clenching it in her fist. Kate still had her hand on my shoulder.

The wait seemed interminable. But finally, the rankings were called out over the loudspeaker.

"In sixth place, from Glenridge Skating Club, Danielle Swaybe …"

I watched as the skaters who received ribbons for sixth through fourth place were called up to claim them. Then the medals began.

"In third place, from Calston Skate, Pamela Denault."

Pamela skated out and stepped onto the low podium that had been set in the middle of the ice.

"In second place …" I heard Amy's breath catch. "… from Richmond Skate Club, Jennie Brewster."

The unexpected words paralyzed me for a moment, before I dredged up a smile and skated out to the podium. I'd beaten Amy so often that losing to her never really occurred to me as a serious possibility, even though I knew our marks had been close. As I stepped up onto the second step, I caught a glimpse of Amy's glowing smile. She was still standing beside Kate, her face transfixed.

"In first place, from Richmond Skate Club … Amy Sehlmeier."

Kate squeezed Amy's shoulder, and a wide, sincere smile spread across Amy's face. She skated out and climbed onto the highest step of the podium. She waved joyfully to the crowd as the first place medal was hung around her neck, and she bent to hug me and Pamela as we congratulated her.

"You skated really great," she whispered.

I smiled. "So did you." The gold-coloured medal around Amy's neck reflected the glare from the rink's bright overhead lights.

"Thanks!" Amy giggled. She couldn't stop smiling.

We stepped down from the podium and skated off the ice. I sat down on one of the lower bleachers and pulled my skate bag out from underneath. I couldn't wait to get into a hot shower. I wiped the ice from my blades, pulling on the rubber skate guards, when my parents and Kate came over.

"Well, I'm telling you, Kate, Jennie had a much higher degree of difficulty than Amy," My dad was saying. "It's not that Amy didn't skate well — she did. But Jennie should have had the higher marks. She completed the routine almost flawlessly."

Kate looked uncomfortable. "Jennie skated very well. And her routine *was* more difficult. But Amy placed higher in the short program, and the judges marked her higher for presentation in the long."

"She did have a lot of flair out there," Dad admitted. "But Jennie's double Axel should have counted for something."

It did, I wanted to say, it counts to *me*. And that's what mattered. After the first few seconds of shock when I placed second to Amy, I discovered that I didn't really care so much about the colour of the medal. I'd tried as hard as I could, even after one of the toughest competition falls of my life, and I had landed the jump that had been a problem for so long.

"I just don't see how they could have marked Amy higher," Mom said. The slight whine in her voice annoyed me. "Jennie was really fabulous."

Kate tried to shrug. "Judged sports are very subjective. Both girls were excellent. It was a hard decision to make."

Mom shook her head. "Well, I can't say I agree with it."

"Mom!" I broke in. "You guys are all missing the point. I don't care where I placed!"

They all looked at me like I had three heads.

"I mean it. Winning is great, but I did my absolute best out there. I *landed* my double Axel. Don't you realize how important that is to me?"

Kate smiled. "You're absolutely right."

I glanced over at Amy, who was surrounded by her parents, some of the kids from school, including Kallana and Kyle, and a handful of skaters who wanted to congratulate her. She looked bright and bubbly — she was laughing, showing a lot of pearly white teeth, and swishing her chiffon skating skirt as she mimed a jump. Her whole personality seemed different.

"I don't want winning to be my only goal," I tried to explain. "I don't want to live and die for every medal I win, and wind up being disappointed if I go home with silver or bronze, or nothing at all. What if

I *do* go to the Olympics some day, and I don't place? Would that mean my whole skating career had been a waste? There's got to be more to it than that."

My parents looked at each other in startled shock.

"When," my dad said slowly, "did we get such a wise daughter?"

Mom sniffled. "Honey, I'm sorry. You're right. And here we are, getting carried away over a few points from the judges. Feeling good about how you performed is more important than any medal."

"Jennie's more than right," Kate said suddenly. "Do you know how many athletes pin all their hopes on the Olympics, or some other huge competition, and work toward it every day of their life for years, only to wind up with the flu, or an injury, or some other reason why they can't perform at their peak on that particular day — and lose? And then feel cheated?" She shook her head. "That's not what sports should be about."

"No," I said. I looked at Amy again. The crowd had departed, and Amy was sitting on the bottom bleacher, her medal in her hand. I knew it meant a lot to her, to finally beat me. But I still felt good about what I'd accomplished.

"Hey, Jennie!" Kyle climbed over the skate bags and jackets that littered the floor in front of the bleachers. "Fantastic skate!"

I grinned. "Thanks. I thought so, too." I stepped away from my parents and Kate to talk to him.

"Hey, by the way, my mom got some tickets for

another figure skating thing tonight. You want to go? She said I could ask you," Kyle said.

Puzzled, I asked. "What figure skating thing?"

"It's some dopey fairy tale or something." Kyle tried hard to keep a straight face.

It took a minute to register. "You don't mean Beauty and the Beast on Ice, with Tara Lipinski, do you?" I said.

"Yeah, I think that's it," Kyle said.

"That's been sold out for weeks!" I shouted. "Of course I'll go!"

Kyle seemed to ignore my outburst. "I don't know if it'll be any good or not," he said, teasing. "We could skip it and play street hockey instead."

"Kyle!"

He grinned. "I'm kidding. Pick you up after supper, okay?"

"Okay." I couldn't help smiling as I watched Kyle bound out of the room. For a moment, I'd forgotten the silver medal hanging around my neck, but as the overhead lights glittered off it, I wrapped my fist around the heavy disk and felt the warm metal in my hand. There would always be another competition, another medal, another performance. That was part of skating.

"Hey, Jennie!" Kyle stuck his head back through the doorway.

I looked up. "Yeah?"

"Don't forget the taco chips."

Other books you'll enjoy in the
Sports Stories series

Basketball
❏ *Queen of the Court* by Michele Martin Bossley #40
What happens when the school's fashion queen winds up on the basketball court?

Figure Skating
❏ *A Stroke of Luck* by Kathryn Ellis #6
Strange accidents are stalking one of the skaters at the Millwood Arena.

❏ *Leap of Faith* by Michele Martin Bossley #36
Amy wants to win at any cost, until an injury makes skating almost impossible. Will she go on?

❏ *Ice Dreams* by Beverly Scudamore #65
Twelve-year-old Maya is a talented figure skater, just as her mother was before she died four years ago. Despite pressure from her family to keep skating, Maya tries to pursue her passion for goaltending.

Swimming
❏ *Water Fight!* by Michele Martin Bossley #14
Josie's perfect sister is driving her crazy, but when she takes up swimming — Josie's sport — it's too much to take.

❏ *Taking a Dive* by Michele Martin Bossley #19
Josie holds the provincial record for the butterfly, but in this sequel to Water Fight! she can't seem to match her own time and might not go on to the nationals.

❏ *Great Lengths* by Sandra Diersch #26
Fourteen-year-old Jessie decides to find out whether the rumours about a new swimmer at her Vancouver club are true.